ALSO BY TOMMY HAYS

Sam's Crossing

In the Family Way

IN THE FAMILY WAY

A Novel

Tommy Hays

RANDOM HOUSE

NEW YORK

This is a work of fiction.
Names, characters, places, and incidents
are the products of the author's imagination or
are used fictitiously. Any resemblance to
actual events, locales, or persons, living
or dead, is entirely coincidental.

Library of Congress Cataloging-in-Publication Data

Hays, Tommy.
In the family way : a novel / Tommy Hays.
p.   cm.
ISBN 0-375-50211-4 (alk. paper)
I. Title.
PS3558.A87515   1999
813'.54—dc21   98-30764   CIP

Printed in the United States of America
on acid-free paper
Random House website address:
www.atrandom.com
2 4 6 8 9 7 5 3
First Edition

For my parents, Tom and Marguerite
—*who encouraged their children to follow their dreams*

For my brother, Chris
—*who dreams beautiful buildings*

For my children, Max and Ruth
—*who returned me to my own childhood*

And for my wife, Connie
—*without whom not one word of this book
could have been written*

ACKNOWLEDGMENTS

I am indebted to Robert Boswell for the critical role he played in the evolution of this book. Other readers who contributed significantly to its shape and content are Joan Aleshire, Sam Hodges, Karen McElmurray, Kris Nord, Kathy Sheldon, and Joan Silber. I want to thank John Skoyles, Dore Hansel, Steve Baker, Dale Davis, and all other family and friends who sustained me.

I want to thank my agent, Jennifer Hengen, who believed in the book, and my editor, Lee Boudreaux, who gave it a good home.

Finally, I want to thank the Arts Alliance of Asheville, North Carolina, for supporting a grateful member of the community.

ʏ

In the Family Way

In the Family Way

TWO WEEKS AFTER MY BROTHER Mitchell was killed, my mother finally emerged from her bedroom, hair un-combed, eyes puffy and wide. She said nothing to us, who watched her cross the floor to the bathroom, where she emptied the medicine cabinet. She stepped into the living room holding a waste can full of medicine bottles and an-nounced that she had become a Christian Scientist.

The year was 1962. I was nine and didn't know what Christian Science was. But I could see it had enabled my mother to walk from her bedroom and speak to us, and I was grateful for that.

She had taken Mitchell's death harder than any of us. She had grown up in a family of early deaths. Her grand-mother had died giving birth to her mother, Grace, who, in turn, had died giving birth to a stillborn daughter. Her father, Jeru, so grieved these losses that he died three years later, at the age of forty-one, of a heart attack. My mother and her brother Charlie then went to live with their great-aunt and great-uncle, Louise and Clem Marsh-banks. Brother and sister, Louise and Clem became my mother's surrogate parents and, eventually, my surrogate grandparents.

Mitchell was almost eight when he was killed, and I was the only witness. Death had made my family conspicuous. We buried Mitchell alongside my grandparents in Springwood, Greenville's downtown cemetery. My mother often visited his grave on her way home from the newspaper, where she worked. She said our grandparents and Mitchell didn't actually die, she claimed no one died. "Death," she was fond of repeating, "is the ultimate illusion."

My father took solace in my mother's discovery of Christian Science. It justified his own religious preoccupations. Ever since his college days, he had read and studied books of the great Eastern religions, but after Mitchell was killed, he immersed himself in them with a new zeal. He resigned from his job at the advertising agency and began to write a novel. He kept strange hours. For him, church became a late-night diner where he discussed the Buddha over a cup of coffee with a road-weary trucker. Mitchell's death drove both my parents to religion: My mother, a Southern Baptist, turned Christian Scientist, and my father, a midwestern Presbyterian, became a Waffle House mystic.

Mitchell's death put me off God. I didn't trust a deity who allowed what had happened to Mitchell in the Moores' field that afternoon. I placed my faith in the pioneers, inventors, and baseball players whose stories I devoured nightly. In my personal sect, the holy trinity was Daniel Boone, Lou Gehrig, and Thomas Alva Edison. Since Mitchell's death I had become obsessed with biographies and read under the covers with a flashlight late into the night, losing myself in the abridged lives of great men.

The nights I couldn't read, when the words sat there on the page, being their secret selves, leading me nowhere, I relived the afternoon Mitchell and I had been playing along the creek bank, in the field next to Uncle Clem and Aunt Louise's house. I see the German shepherd, its broken chain trailing behind, tear across the creek from the direction of Colored Town. The dog charges through the high grass, not barking, not even growling. We run, but I am heavy and slow. I might be screaming. When Mitchell sees the German shepherd gain on me, he drops back, and I run past him. He holds out his opened hand to the dog. I hear him speak; the words seem to be whispered in my ear. "Here, boy. Come here, boy. It's all right." Mitchell has pulled off this trick before, and I have a second to believe it will work before the dog takes him down. Uncle Clem appears at the edge of the field with his .22. Two Negro boys splash through the creek, calling the dog. The rifle fires in the air, but the dog doesn't run. Uncle Clem beats it off Mitchell with the butt of the gun, then shoots it three times.

My last memory of Mitchell is him standing there, hand out, palm up, offering himself as he always offered himself to everyone and everything. That is how Aunt Louise said I should remember him. Never mind that I had my back to him, that I was running and could not have seen it. She said I should hang on to that image and forget about afterward because that was no longer Mitchell.

ONE MINUTE I HAD RUN DOWN the Donaldson Elementary steps, tossing a year's worth of papers into the air, the next minute I trudged back up those same stairs, lugging a new notebook heavy with blank Blue Horse paper.

The summer of 1963 had flown away with the lightning bugs.

Now I had turned ten. The past year had given my family a little distance from Mitchell's death, but loss remained a permanent guest in our household. If anyone had mentioned the word "healing," I would have assumed they were referring to one of my mother's ardent appeals to Divine Science. It would be the year that too much happened, and, by being too much, was just enough.

I trace the first strands of these events, or at least my awareness of them, back to my first day of school. I had felt a cold coming on for a couple of days, something I was especially conscious of since my mother's new religion complicated the simplest illness. To be sick became, at least to some extent, our fault—the result of our listening to Mortal Mind. On this morning, I had awakened with a sore throat and a stuffy nose.

Usually by the end of summer, the familiar landscape of my neighborhood had become claustrophobic. I had explored every creek, shinnied every tree, and raced my bike down the same streets so often I could have steered in my sleep. I was usually more than ready for school to begin and looked forward to accompanying my mother to the Lewis Plaza Pharmacy the week before to buy supplies. I liked the sharp smell of a new notebook and the smooth feel of a set of number 2 pencils.

On this particular morning, as I slumped at the breakfast table, picking at my Cocoa Puffs, I suppressed a cough, set down the book I had been reading, and gazed out the window. Outside, the world looked bright and already hot. It might have been the end of my summer, but September in Greenville, South Carolina, could be stifling.

Ahead of me loomed fifth grade, like one of those long, dark culverts that we would stand at the mouth of, dare each other to enter, and then crawl a couple of yards into before a web broke across our face or our hand fell on something slippery and alive, sending us scrambling back toward the light, our screams echoing in the chilly dankness.

Taller than our fathers, Vessie Hawkins ruled Donaldson Elementary fifth grade with her bony index finger, flicking children's ears. Generations of children had weathered her classroom, including my mother. It was my turn.

"You hasn't touched your cereal." Della tapped my book. She wore dangling gold earrings and half a dozen bracelets as she cleared the breakfast dishes. Every morning at eight o'clock she arrived, wielding her suitcase-size pocketbook and smelling of perfume and bus diesel.

Della Williams had worked for us since I had been an infant, when my mother, who preferred composing birth announcements to changing diapers, returned to her job as editor of the society section of the Greenville *Piedmont*. Della raised all three of us: me, Mitchell, and Henry, the youngest. Mitchell had been her favorite. At the funeral she screamed his name and draped herself over his coffin. "Why You take him, Lord? They say You merciful! Where Your mercy?" She stamped her feet and snapped her head back. Hundreds of solemn white people looked on in astonishment as Della collapsed on her knees beside the coffin. "Don't go, Mitchell! Please, please don't leave us, honey!" Her head jerked and her eyes rolled back. I remember being afraid she might be dying as well. My father and Uncle Charlie had to carry her to a chair, where she hummed to herself and swayed. I sensed disapproval from the mourners; how tacky for a family to be out-grieved by the maid.

"You sniffling, Jeru," Della said. Although my name is spelled with an *e*, it is pronounced with a long *a* like "jay-bird," which is what Uncle Clem sometimes called me.

"You catching a cold?" Della picked up my father's empty plate.

I held my finger to my lips and gestured toward the bathroom, where my mother's hair spray hissed. Henry sat across from me, eating his Alpha-Bits and swirling a jelly jar that contained two pink pigeon feet suspended in alcohol. Uncle Clem had given it to him. Henry collected bones, shells, dead insects—the remains of most anything. Today was his first day of kindergarten. He would attend the same Episcopal kindergarten I had attended down-town.

I blew my nose into my Kit Carson handkerchief.

"Ask your daddy to give you something for that cold," Della whispered, and backed into the kitchen door with an armful of dishes. "And get the pigeon toes off the table, Henry."

We ate at a small table in the den, because the dining-room table felt too big after Mitchell's death. The den was paneled in pickled oak, giving the room an algae-green glow. At the other end was a squarish brown Naugahyde couch and an easy chair that faced the black-and-white TV.

"Why do you keep looking at me?" Henry had glanced down at his shirt. "Did I spill some cereal?"

How could I tell him that he was growing into Mitchell's likeness? He had the same slender build, the same curly black hair, the same crooked nose. He was even wearing Mitchell's short-sleeved shirt, his khaki shorts, and his red PF Flyers. Sometimes my father alluded to reincarnation, how someone could be an ant in one life and a bird in the next, but I wondered could one brother come back as another?

"Are you thinking something?" Henry set down the jar and ate another bite of cereal.

"It's complicated." I wiped my nose with my handkerchief.

"You don't tell me things." Henry shook his spoon at me.

"I tell you lots of things," I said, suppressing another cough.

"No, you don't," Henry said.

Our mother clicked out of the bathroom in her high heels. A cloud of Clairol hung over her. "Did I hear you cough?" She pressed my forehead.

"Allergies." I dabbed my nose.

Henry picked up his cereal bowl and swallowed the last of the milk. He pushed back his chair, grabbed the jar, and trotted to the bathroom.

"You aren't eating." My mother touched my cereal bowl. When I didn't answer, she pulled a chair beside mine and sat. "Miss Hawkins is a good teacher." She frowned to herself. "Strict, but a very good teacher. I survived her." She put her arms around me. "Nothing is going to happen to you." Her eyes reddened. For the past year her eyes had reddened without warning, in the checkout line at the A&P or at the counter at the Sanitary Bakery or in the boys' department at Ivey's.

My mother was a handsome woman, with long eyelashes and full red lips, but, after Mitchell died, the wrinkles on her forehead deepened, and her hair grayed. Even though she had regained most of her weight, her cheeks had stayed slightly sunken. Her features had been striking on her, but on me, a pale, overweight, ten-year-old boy, such feminine features were a hardship. It didn't help that I had inherited her thick, straight hair, which she insisted that I part severely with a wet comb.

I also had inherited my mother's passion for sweets— the reason we shopped for my pants in the husky section. My mother's last memory of her own mother had been of sharing a sundae with her at the fountain of Carpenter Brothers, a drugstore downtown. Dessert was a kind of love, and it came to us as chocolate eclairs, Neapolitan ice cream, and thick wedges of coconut cake. Yet I was the only one in my family who was overweight. The others practiced moderation, but I believed there were few things in life you could count on, an Oreo being one of them.

"Miss Hawkins cannot hurt you," my mother said, stroking the back of my head.

I pulled out my handkerchief and blew my nose, feeling betrayed by my body.

"I want us to pray silently," she said, bowing her head and closing her eyes.

I folded my handkerchief and put it in my pocket.

"Bow your head." She kept her eyes closed.

I bowed my head. Off in the bathroom, Henry was making a loud production of brushing his teeth, gargling and spitting. Dishes clinked in the kitchen sink as Della rinsed and stacked them in the drain. Beneath us, my father typed.

Through my half-open eyes, I studied the front yard with its great oaks, its bowed dogwoods, and, off to the side, Mitchell's tree, a wide magnolia whose low limbs we climbed and whose dense leaves formed a cool, dim re-treat from the afternoon sun and kept us dry during sum-mer showers. In July, ivory stars blossomed on the end of the branches, giving off a too-sweet smell. In August, the petals dropped away, leaving grenades of seeds that even-tually fell to the ground. The magnolia had been among Mitchell's favorite places; a perfect spy tree from which we could see out but into which the neighborhood could not see.

Past our yard was Afton Avenue, a block-long street in a middle-class neighborhood, whose boundaries were so in-grained in our interior maps that simply by crossing cer-tain streets we entered other worlds altogether. This worked both ways. Occasionally, a group of Negro chil-dren passed through our neighborhood—a motley band of explorers, toting big sticks and keeping an eye out for dogs.

After a couple of minutes of silent prayer, my mother opened her eyes and laid her hand on my knee. "Better?"

I nodded, suppressing a sneeze, which, according to Roger Avant across the street, obliterated several million brain cells. She straightened my collar. She started to stand but then put her hand to her stomach. She lowered her head onto the table, closing her eyes. She was having an-other of her stomachaches, which she said weren't actu-ally stomachaches but Error.

I ran to the kitchen, told Della, who stubbed out her cig-arette, poured a glass of milk, and handed it to me. She fol-lowed me to the dining room. My mother, still looking pale, sat in the chair, leafing through *Science and Health with Key to the Scriptures*, a small green book she kept in her purse.

My mother took the glass of milk but set it on the table. "Already better," she said.

"Your ulcer again?" Della asked, wiping her hands on her apron.

"It doesn't feel like that," she said, closing the book. "My ulcer hasn't bothered me in some time."

"What do it feel like?"

My mother opened her mouth to speak but then paused. The two women studied each other. My mother laid her hand on her stomach, almost reverently. "A little nauseous," she said, lowering her voice.

Della straightened the chairs around the table, while I spooned up the last of my cereal. "You was like this yesterday morning, too," said Della. "Maybe you ought to call Dr. Norton."

"I don't believe in doctors."

Della looked at me. "Honey, carry your bowl on out to the kitchen." They didn't resume talking until I had disappeared behind the kitchen door. I set the bowl in the sink and started back to the den but paused just inside the door, cracking it slightly.

"You isn't in the family way, is you?" Della whispered. "Dr. Norton say you shouldn't have more."

My mother glanced out the window at Mrs. Avant, who was backing down her driveway in her green Peugeot. Trudy Avant was the only other mother on our street who worked full-time. "This is ridiculous," my mother said. "All this excitement over a queasy stomach."

"Yes, ma'am." Della lowered her eyelids the way she did when she knew more than she was saying, which was most of the time. As a Negro maid to a Southern white family, she was forever conscious of the very fine line between showing her concern and being what might have been considered impertinent.

"Dr. Norton is a good man." My mother looked calmly at Della. "But his is the voice of Mortal Mind."

"Mrs. Lamb, is you saying you—"

"If you trust in God, then He is the only precaution you need." As my mother whispered this, she grimaced and held her stomach.

"Do Mr. Lamb know?"

"I haven't quite gotten around to telling him."

Della picked up the morning paper and folded it, not looking at my mother. While I did not understand precisely what they were talking about, I understood the gist of their conversation—my mother had thrown out something else in the name of Christian Science, but Della thought this was something essential.

I stepped into the den, and the two women looked at me, wondering if I had been listening, since I was known to on occasion. Luckily, Henry ran out of his room, carrying the little red satchel that had once been mine. "Come on, Mama."

"We're late," said my mother, glancing at her watch. She watched Della disappear into the kitchen, without another word.

"Come on, Mama," Henry said, tugging her arm. "I don't want to be late on my first day."

She snatched her briefcase by the door, grabbed Henry's hand, and hurried out. She turned around halfway down the sidewalk. "Miss Hawkins is the Divine Reflection of God."

I waved from the open doorway, cats running outside between my legs. After Mitchell's death, I had not wanted my family out of my sight, fearing that I would never see them again. And it was with renewed dread that I watched my mother and my brother pull away in the Chevrolet.

I went to my room and shouldered my knapsack. I picked up the worn pocketknife on my dresser, a gift from Uncle Clem, who said he had had it since World War I (even though he had not participated in the war). The knife had accompanied me every day that summer. I slipped it into my pocket, along with a lucky marble and a flint arrowhead that had been Mitchell's. For the past year, I had loaded my pockets with talismans. On the day Mitchell died, his pockets had been empty.

I PAUSED OUTSIDE MY FATHER'S OFFICE DOOR, my stomach tightening. I didn't like to bother him when he was writing. I pressed my ear to the door. My father could type faster than any father in the neighborhood. I was proud of this. Some fathers built things, other fathers labored in their yards, and other fathers tinkered with cars. My father typed. And he typed with such speed and confidence that to sit and listen outside his office door was to know that something profound was being accomplished.

As I opened the door, a cloud of smoke curled toward me, a smoky finger beckoning me to enter. My father's office was a spare, paneled room that he had had built after Mitchell died. Since the office was part of the basement, it was cool even on the hottest days. Drawings of women covered the walls. No bodies. Just faces. Different faces, but all sharing the same serene expression. Whenever I went into my father's office, I felt self-conscious under their contemplative gazes. My father had sketched these women for as long as I could remember. He sketched them like doodles, without thinking. He sketched them on restaurant napkins, on paper towels, on pages of the phone book, and in the margins of magazines. He didn't use models or even photographs. They simply took form under his pen.

My father sat behind his desk in his coat and tie, which he wore every day even though his going to work consisted of descending a flight of stairs. He squinted at a piece of paper in his typewriter, a lighted cigarette dangled from his mouth. Crumpled sheets of paper covered his desk, and the trash can beside his desk overflowed. At one corner of his desk was a neat stack of several hundred pages, one year's work.

I stood in the doorway with my knapsack.

"A short-order cook at the Waffle House says that our culture puts so much emphasis on the outer that we have become a society of walking husks," he said, stubbing his cigarette in his ashtray and squinting at me.

"I'm heading out." I blew my nose into my handkerchief.

"Where to?" He frowned at the typewriter.

"It's the first day of school."

"Summer is over?" He looked out his window, which opened onto the concrete driveway and the backyard beyond, with its rusted swing set. "We ought to move to the Keys."

"Don't they have school there?" I asked.

My father had always talked about Florida, not so much as a place (he had never been) but as a concept of uninterrupted summer and palm trees.

"Can I borrow a pencil?" I asked.

He handed me two sharpened ones. "Pronounced *pencil.*"

"Pen-cil." I felt the sides of my mouth stretch in an ugly grimace.

As the lone Yankee in our family, my father had fought to straighten our vowels and uncurl our consonants. He conducted pronunciation exercises, having us say words such as "pen" and "tennis" until the sides of our mouths ached. I grew up convinced that Northerners talked so fast because it was physically painful for them to speak.

I lingered in the doorway, looking back at my father. He was already typing. I started to leave, but my coughing stopped me.

"That doesn't sound good," my father said. "Maybe you should stay home?"

"I can't miss the first day of school."

My father took out his key chain and unlocked a desk drawer. He hesitated. "She's gone?" He opened the deep drawer, which glittered with colored medicine bottles: Pepto-Bismol, milk of magnesia, Bufferin, Alka-Seltzer, and enough Ex-Lax to blow out an army. He lifted a bottle of Robitussin, wiped off a big sticky spoon with a piece of typing paper, and filled it. He held it out to me.

"Isn't that grown-up medicine?" I eyed the red syrup.

" 'Grown-up' is a state of mind."

The medicine burned going down. He put the Robitussin and the spoon away, locked the drawer, and lit another cigarette.

I saw a small, opened blue envelope beside his typewriter. The writing on the envelope was a shaky cursive. I had noticed an occasional blue envelope in the pile of mail on the foyer table, always with the same handwriting, and although there was never a return address, it was always postmarked Wilmington, North Carolina. The blue letters had begun arriving not long after Mitchell's death, and I somehow had enough sense not to ask about them. They disappeared from the stack of mail before my mother came home from work.

"Anything else?" My father took a long drag on his cigarette, his eyes on the sheet of paper in the typewriter.

I lifted a snow-scene paperweight off his desk. Mitchell had given it to him one Christmas. It was of a tiny house with a picket fence and with even tinier figures, which I took to be children playing in the snow. I shook it. "Didn't my grandmother die having a baby?" I watched my father's face through the snowy landscape.

"Life comes at a high price on your mother's side of the family," he said, not looking up.

"And didn't Mama almost die having Henry?"

"Henry had his own ideas about how he should make his entrance." He typed a few words.

"And didn't Dr. Norton say it would be bad if she had any more?"

"She can't have more." He blew cigarette smoke over the typewriter. "Why this sudden interest in procreation?"

I looked through the paperweight at my father's face. My coughing had stopped, but I felt woozy. "If Mama doesn't believe in doctors, how come she takes the cats to the vet?"

"Because they can't read *Science and Health*." He had started typing again, his lips moving with the words he wrote, his cigarette bouncing. I set down the paperweight and started out the door.

"Jeru?"

"Yes, sir?"

He didn't stop typing. "If you meet the Buddha on the road, kill him."

"Yes, sir." I climbed the stairs, said good-bye to Della, and walked down our front walk, looking back, knowing, in a way I hadn't before Mitchell's death, that each leaving was an incalculable risk. I sat down on the curb and waited for Roger to come out.

The neighborhood shimmered around me, the day's heat already rising from the pavement. The air smelled heavy, and cicadas droned monotonously in the trees. It was summer, and it was not. I felt light-headed, hovering over myself. I was in the middle of my first out-of-body experience, brought on by an overdose of Robitussin.

I reached into my pocket, making sure my knife was there in case I had to swiftly dispatch the Buddha. My father often talked to me about metaphysical things that, as far as I know, he never talked to anyone else about, and although I seldom understood, it made me feel trusted.

Greenville seemed an obscure and unlikely place for my father. I knew little about him, considering I was his son. He had grown up in a suburb of Chicago, attended the University of Illinois, and served in the Merchant Marine on the Great Lakes—from big city to big school to big lakes. How he had made his way from the Midwest to a textile town at the foot of the Blue Ridge Mountains was a mystery. Still, I felt privileged that he had traveled such a distance to be our father.

The other thing I knew was that he and my mother had met at the *Piedmont*. He had been a sportswriter and she a copy editor. They had argued over a sentence he had written. He was fond of saying that I owed my existence to a misplaced modifier.

As I sat on the curb, high on cold medicine, I felt a stab of guilt for not telling my family what I knew, which was that something terrible, even catastrophic, was going to happen, again. Whatever I felt in my stomach (had felt for some time) was the same falling-out-of-bed sensation that came over me before Henry was born breech, before Uncle Clem fell from the ladder while painting Aunt Louise's ceiling and broke his ankle, before the German shepherd snapped his chain.

It was not lost on me that by expecting the worst every breathing moment, I backed into prophecy once in a while. Still, I trusted my stomach, having decided that the heart, at least in our family, was a fickle organ that would quit on you without a minute's notice.

I STOOD WHEN ROGER AVANT TRUDGED down his driveway, his knapsack on his back. Roger had grown up in a houseful of older siblings and was knowledgeable beyond his years. He was my source on everything from Santa Claus to girls. Roger was also my bridge between home and school—the one person who knew me in both places.

A slim boy with dark circles under his eyes, Roger walked with his shoulders stooped. He planned to be an astrophysicist, a brain surgeon, or a stunt-car driver.

We started down Afton Avenue in the direction of school, anticipating what lay ahead. Before, Mitchell had walked between us. He and Roger had been good friends. If there was a pileated woodpecker high in a pine tree or a praying mantis crouched in an azalea, they would point it out. To be with one of them had been educational, to be with both had been exhausting.

Roger's parents were separated. I didn't understand how anyone could leave Roger's mother—a pretty, fair-skinned woman who was a nurse at Greenville General Hospital. When I read about Clara Barton in a biography from the school library, I pictured Mrs. Avant in the fields, tending wounded soldiers.

Dr. Avant was thin with a sharp nose, caterpillar eyebrows, and eyes that skewered your soul. He hardly ever smiled, and when he did, it looked all wrong. He was a psychiatrist, of an exotic profession associated with strait-jackets and padded cells. It shocked the neighborhood when he walked out on his wife since it had been expected, even hoped, that she would leave him.

The walk to school was ten blocks, about a mile and a half of streets like my own, all lined with oaks whose roots bulged like thick tentacles over the sidewalk. Most of the houses were single story and brick. Almost every yard was bordered by substantial hedges of hemlock, holly, or boxwood. The nicer the houses, the taller the hedges. Behind the hedges was thick, lush fescue. In places where there was too much shade, ivy owned the ground. It was so humid and rainy in Greenville that the vegetation had a belligerence about it. Most people devoted their weekends to keeping their yards in check.

As we neared school, we passed more children walking with their knapsacks and satchels and talking excitedly among themselves. "Take a ride on the green trolley," said one girl, nudging her brother into a prickly juniper bush that all but blocked the sidewalk.

Too soon, Donaldson Elementary, a rectangular redbrick box, appeared ahead. Its substantial walls had been laid after World War I by men back from the trenches, with fortresses still very much on their minds. Last year, home had been hard, and school—with my kind teacher—had provided refuge. But with Miss Hawkins, I didn't know what to expect.

I stared at the building, turning Mitchell's arrowhead over in my pocket. "If something happens to me in there, you can have all my books about the presidents."

"Don't be so melodramatic," said Roger, who often sounded like his psychiatrist father and used language that I didn't quite understand.

We passed the playground—a dusty field, a sliding board too hot to slide on, a seesaw, swings with hard wooden seats and a water fountain made from a long iron pipe with holes. The water dribbled out of the holes and was almost impossible to drink unless you pressed your fingers over a couple of other holes. The teachers didn't think this was good hygiene.

Beyond the woods at the edge of the playground was Maybar, a Negro neighborhood. It did not strike me as the least bit odd that no Negro children attended Donaldson even though they lived next door. Sometimes we passed them walking to their bus stop, from where they rode to their elementary school across town, and the only thing I recall wondering was, What were they learning that we were not?

At Donaldson, children arrived from two general directions: our side of Augusta Road or the other side. The children from the other side lived in the Mill's Mill section—blocks of simple, white clapboard houses that radiated outward from the mill. The houses had originally been rented to mill workers, but the mill, which manufactured cotton textiles, had fallen on hard times and had sold the houses. Mill's Mill was a poorer parallel universe.

Our principal, Wilfred Keener, a short, rotund, white-haired man with a cigar butt permanently wedged in the corner of his mouth, presided from the top of the school steps, placing his hand on each child's head, like a priest giving his blessing. Teachers liked him because he kept discipline. We children liked him because he never seemed angry, even when he paddled us.

Chalk and sweat were the first things we smelled as we crossed the worn wooden floors, which creaked with our weight. The hall was an oven, the building having been closed up all summer. Miss Hawkins towered outside the doorway of her classroom, greeting students. I had observed her from the safety of the fourth grade, but this morning I was struck by her homeliness.

Roger blanched when Miss Hawkins waved him over. Here was the woman he had heard horror stories about from his brothers and sister. I feared he might run, and if he did, I would be close behind.

She took his arm and said, "I don't bite."

"That's about all she doesn't do," whispered Norma Jones into my ear. Norma was a wiry, dark-haired girl who lived in Mill's Mill. She had started Donaldson in the middle of last year. She had moved to Greenville with her mother, who had been transferred from a Belk department store in North Carolina to the Belk in downtown Greenville. Her father, a plumber, had died two years ago.

"How was your summer?" Norma asked.

I put my finger to my lips, nodding toward Miss Hawkins, who was smoothing a name tag onto Roger's chest. "I taught your brothers and your sister. They were good students but they were brooders. It is one thing to be thoughtful, another to brood. One is selfless, the other self-centered."

Roger beat a path to a desk in the back row.

Her gray head swiveled toward me. "Good morning. You are Muriel Thompson's boy."

"Muriel *Lamb*."

She placed her bony hand on my back. "I taught your mother twenty years ago. She was a smart girl, a good speller as I recall. Writes for the *Piedmont* now." She tapped her brow. "Your family has had a difficult year."

"A nigger dog attacked his brother," said Ricky McIntire, who had just come in the door. He was a skinny, freckled-faced boy who was already an old man. Like Norma, he was from Mill's Mill. "It was all over the paper."

"You will not use that word in my classroom." Miss Hawkins took a step toward Ricky.

"Jeru seen it hisself," Ricky said. "Seen that big old dog light into his brother—"

Norma jabbed Ricky in the ribs.

Miss Hawkins leaned over and smoothed my name tag onto my shirt pocket. "Mrs. Bemans says you are imaginative." Her breath was a stale combination of peppermint and mothballs. "Imagination runs in your family. Your mother was the same way." She leaned closer. "I will tell you what I told her twenty years ago. Imagination has its place, and it is not in my classroom."

She greeted most of us in this way, connecting us with a mother or a father, a sister or a brother, an aunt or an uncle. There was hardly a child for whom she hadn't taught at least one of our relations over the past fifty years and with whom she pegged our personalities. What surprised us was how easily we slipped into our predecessor's shoes. In a way, it felt reassuring to carry on the family neurosis.

I started toward a desk near Roger's, but Miss Hawkins didn't release my arm. "Maybe you could spell 'imagination' for us?"

"Right now?"

"No time like the present."

I sighed. " 'Imagination' . . . *I, m, a, g,* . . ." I paused.

"Yes?" I could feel Miss Hawkins's finger at my ear. I hadn't been in her classroom five minutes and I was about to be flicked.

"*i,*" whispered a voice right behind me.

"*i, n, a, t, i, o, n.*"

Miss Hawkins scowled. I was sure she had heard the voice, but she clapped her hands. "Correct."

I scurried to a seat, grateful to Norma, who at great personal risk had spared me Miss Hawkins's finger. Now Norma stood at the front of the class.

"Mrs. Bemans tells me you are one of the best students she has ever had."

"I ain't that smart." Norma shrugged.

" 'Am not,' " Miss Hawkins corrected.

The lean little girl wiped her nose on the sleeve of her blouse. It was common knowledge that Norma had scored the highest IQ in the county. In the four months I had been in school with her, I had never known her to miss a math problem or misspell a word.

Norma joined Roger and me in the back row, sitting in the desk next to mine. A warm breeze blew through the large fold-down windows. A wasp bumped against the ceiling.

Miss Hawkins clapped her hands. "Class, please stand and recite the Pledge of Allegiance." She faced the small flag that hung beneath the portrait of George Washington, whose benevolent gaze sometimes seemed to border on distraction.

With a scraping of chairs, we placed our hands over our hearts. It was going to be a long year.

"I pledge allegiance to the flag of the United States of America," we droned, "and to the republic for which it stands, one nation under God . . ." Under God? My mother couldn't be right. How could Miss Hawkins be the reflection of God? One look at this old woman and you knew she came from the underworld. She wasn't the reflection of anything. She was a shade, a shade with fingernails.

Norma laid her hand on my knee and whispered, "You're taller," in her scratchy voice. She smelled like toast.

CHAPTER TWO

My Aunt
and Thomas Edison

UNCLE CLEM WORKED THE TOMATO PLANTS at the far end of the row, tying them with Aunt Louise's old, misshapen stockings. I hoed crabgrass and dandelions among the last of the corn. I knew the time was not far off when the weeds would finally have their way with my uncle's garden.

It was a muggy Saturday afternoon in mid-September, two weeks into school. I was spending the weekend with Louise and Clem. Their two-story, cedar-sided house, Clem's garden, and the abandoned college campus across the street were my private domain, even more so after Mitchell's death. Henry never shared my interest in Louise and Clem's, and whenever I spent the night, he stayed home.

Louise and Clem were an unlikely pair. Aunt Louise had been among the first women in Greenville to graduate from college, while Uncle Clem never completed sixth grade. Aunt Louise had worked forty years as secretary to the president of the college, while Uncle Clem had had a number of odd jobs in mills and factories. But Clem could never stay on anywhere and lived with (some would suggest lived *off*) his sister.

In all fairness, Clem did design and construct their house. He built the chicken coop and the toolshed and cultivated the bountiful garden. In the basement he built a workshop—a dim room that smelled of sawdust and chewing tobacco, where he repaired lamps, fans, radios, clocks, pieces of furniture, even our toys.

Clem was a short, squat man, and wore a cap that seemed surgically attached to his head. From the time I had been old enough to walk, I had accompanied him out to the half-acre garden. We would wind through the beds, past the empty chicken coop to the toolshed. He would swing open the door and motion to the hoes, spades, and shovels as if he expected them to float out of the shed and work the garden themselves.

I would take down a light, smooth-handled hoe that over the years became *my* hoe. Clem taught me to dig beds, fertilize, plant, and water, but weeding was my specialty. I dispatched wild onions, chickweed, and crabgrass. I prided myself on how well I handled my hoe, having learned from Clem that the key to successful weeding was patience and a willingness to follow all the roots.

On this particular Saturday afternoon, I had worked one row and started another when I nearly brought my hoe down on a large snake, the color of dead leaves. It was rigid, ready. I froze, my bare legs within easy striking distance. It flicked its tongue, testing the air, getting a reading on my warmth. Its diamond-shaped head made its mouth appear to be pulled back in a leer. Years passed. Then, finally, it slid leisurely away, curve by curve, until it disappeared between the plants, leaving a dank odor.

Clem was stooped over a tomato plant at the end of the row. I stared where the snake had been. "Clem!" I yelled.

Hard of hearing, he continued tying a large plant, bent with several nearly ripe tomatoes.

"Clem!"

He lifted his head, cupping his hand to his ear.

"Copperhead!" I held my arms as far apart as I could.

He dropped the garden stakes and limped over, grabbing the hoe from me. With the hoe raised, he hobbled between the rows, nudging corn stalks, beating asparagus bushes, lifting squash leaves. His limp had worsened, and Aunt Louise's arthritis had become so severe she had to use her cane more often.

Clem stopped in the middle of the lima beans. He lifted the hoe over his head and brought it down hard. He brought it down again. I walked over, careful not to step on bean plants. The thick, headless body of the copperhead writhed in the dirt. He prodded the leering head with the hoe. "Be on the lookout for his widow," he said.

"His widow?"

"If you kill one snake, more than likely his widow is in the neighborhood."

The snake had already begun to slow its writhing, flopping in the dirt. I couldn't take my eyes off its mottled brown body. Clem lifted it with the hoe, and I followed him to the back of the garden, where a creek divided their property from that of a Negro shack with a small fenced garden beside it. A small dog on a chain yapped from across the creek.

Clem dropped the snake into the creek, watching it twitch on a flat rock. Setting the hoe on his shoulder, he followed my gaze across the creek to the shack and the barking dog. He sighed. "Yeah, Blakely got hisself a little one. Looks like a terrier mutt. Some nerve to have any kind of dog after what we all been through." Clem put his hand on my head.

Mr. Blakely was an elderly Negro who had lived behind Aunt Louise and Uncle Clem since before my mother had been born. It was his German shepherd that had killed Mitchell. Before the incident, Uncle Clem and Mr. Blakely had been, if not close, at least amiable neighbors. They called out to each other while working their gardens or stood on opposite sides of the creek, trading advice on the best way to grow pole beans or on how to discourage snails. Mr. Blakely always greeted Mitchell and me as well. This ease between the two men was why we had always felt comfortable playing along the creek.

I stared through the fence, seeing Mr. Blakely's house, which was too still and the windows too dark. No sign of life except for the dog. I felt a familiar sadness. My fingers curled around the fence.

"You come on in a minute, Jaybird," Clem said in a quiet voice. He went back to the garden.

I leaned against the fence post and watched the house. Mitchell and I used to go through the gate that connected the garden to the Moores' field. We played along the bank where there wasn't any fence. We threw rocks into the creek. Once in a while, if we didn't see Mr. Blakely or one of his grandchildren, we pelted the sleeping German shepherd chained where the little dog was chained now. If we hit him, he would bark and gnash his teeth, jerking at the chain. We never thought of throwing rocks as cruel. It was an experiment—to see if the chain would hold. And it had, for years.

I walked to the top of the garden and picked up my hoe. Clem was tying another tomato plant and whistling his rhythmless, airy whistle. I looked twice before stepping anywhere, ensuring that I wouldn't bring my foot down on the copperhead's widow. As soon as I started weeding, I forgot about the snake and about Mitchell, losing myself completely in what I was doing.

Louise called us in before dark. We hung our tools in the shed. Lately, it had struck me as sad to put the tools away. I latched the door shut. Clem shook a cigarette from a pack in his shirt pocket.

"What happens when people die?" I asked.

"Not a whole lot." He struck a match on the toolshed door.

"Where do they go?"

"Six feet under." He cupped his hands over the match, lit a cigarette, shook out the match, and tossed it onto the ground.

We started up the path, through the garden. Uncle Clem and I had had this exchange many times. He claimed death was an endless sleep, a notion that seemed unimaginative but hadn't really bothered me until Mitchell died. The thought of my brother sound asleep in the middle of the day was not only disturbing, it was wrong. Mitchell had been an early riser, up before the rest of us, outside riding his bike or perched in the magnolia with his binoculars, watching for birds.

Uncle Clem and I stopped by the goldfish pond. Bright orange fish kissed the surface. I looked across the garden, which appeared greener and lusher at twilight. The heavy smell of bread blew from Claussen's Bakery, which was only one block away.

"Don't go into a nursing home," I said as I dropped a small stick into the water and watched a goldfish nibble it. "I heard Mama talking to Daddy about it the other night."

"Muriel is a good woman, but she is willful, a lot like your Grandma Grace," Clem said, putting his arm around me, using me as support as we climbed the back steps.

"What was Grandma Grace like?"

"She used to spring the chipmunk traps I set. Hid my gun so I couldn't shoot pigeons." He nodded back toward the creek. "Would have given me down the road for that." It was understood that we wouldn't tell my mother about Uncle Clem's killing the snake. She honored all living creatures, no matter how dangerous. Had a Bengal tiger wandered into our backyard, she would have gone out, spoken to it, and served it her cupboard of cat food. Mitchell had been the same way, which was why he hadn't run from the dog.

Aunt Louise was in the kitchen, pouring iced tea. Clem and I washed at the kitchen sink. We told her about the copperhead. She kept putting food on the table without saying a word or even glancing up at us. She was using her cane, so she had to make several trips.

Clem and I frowned at each other. He slid onto his seat at the table, which was tucked into a nook. Uncle Clem made one last attempt to impress her. "If we'd stepped on it, a bite from that big of a snake would have had us up at Mackey's for sure." Mackey's was Greenville's funeral home for white people.

Aunt Louise slid in next to me, propped her cane against the wall, held out her hands for the blessing, and bowed her head. She was a small woman with plain features and thick-lensed glasses, which she wore on a chain around her neck. Her shoes were the substantial, lace-up, square-heeled shoes of elderly women.

She began the blessing, "We thank You for this food You set before us. Help Mr. Khrushchev and the president come to an understanding. Please find sustenance for the starving children in Africa and India." Her blessings often started out global. "And please watch over Jeru's unborn brother or sister. In Jesus' name we pray." When I opened my eyes, she was looking at me over her glasses.

"Come again?" Clem said.

"Muriel called," she said. "She's expecting."

"I thought she wasn't supposed to have another one." Clem bit into a chicken leg. "Won't they have to cut her open again?"

"Clem." Louise shifted her eyes toward me.

He pointed a knife at me. "Sis, you can't coddle the boy. By the time you and me was his age, we'd seen a dozen young 'uns brought into the world."

"Did they have to cut Mama open to get Henry out?" I asked.

Louise narrowed her eyes at Clem. She turned to me. "It's called a cesarean. Your mother doesn't want one this time. She believes God has healed her." She passed me a plate full of biscuits. "And perhaps He has."

Clem gave a noncommittal shrug as he spooned lima beans onto his plate. We ate in silence, the weight of this news sinking in. As always, Clem was the first to finish. He pushed his plate back and lit a cigarette. Then he said

to Aunt Louise, "If you have an in with the big man upstairs, you might better put in a call."

"I have been praying."

"I don't mean for Muriel. Jeru says he heard them talking nursing home again."

Louise sat back. "We can't take care of ourselves. I hob-
ble around here, hardly able to prepare a meal, and you
have trouble getting across the room when your ankle
swells. But every time Muriel hires someone to help, you
run them off."

"Those women was all no-'count help."

"Those women were good housekeepers."

"You haven't been talking to Louise about that Autumn
Care, have you?"

"I don't want to be a burden."

"Louise, the least they can do is let us finish out our
days in our own home." Clem stabbed out his cigarette in
the mortar shell ashtray that always sat on the table. He
slid out of his seat and limped into the den, which doubled
as his bedroom. We heard the TV come on.

"He is worse than a child." Louise waved her hand in
the direction of the den. "Let's get out those lemon tarts
your mama brought."

I cleared the dishes while she lifted a white bakery box
out of the refrigerator and brought it to the table.

"I could take care of y'all," I said, sitting back down. "I
could live here."

Aunt Louise didn't reply, but the way the yellowed clock
over the stove continued to scratch out time with its second hand told me what a foolish thing I had proposed.

She untied the string, lifted out a lemon tart with
whipped cream, and set it on my plate. These were

among my favorite desserts from the Sanitary Bakery, whose unappetizing name harked back to an earlier, less sanitary time.

Aunt Louise took a tart for herself. "Would you prefer a little brother or a little sister?"

"Brother." I didn't dare say it, but I didn't want a *new* brother; I wanted my old one back. I bit into the tart, tasting in one bite the sweetness of the whipped cream and the bitter lemon filling.

After we finished dessert, we washed the dishes and went into the den. Clem sat on his cot, which was covered with an old wool army blanket, his elbows propped on his card table as he watched the small black-and-white TV across the room. I sat beside him.

"We did the dishes," Aunt Louise said, sitting in the stuffed chair. "Without any help from our chief bottle washer."

Uncle Clem didn't take his eyes off the TV.

The theme music for *Saturday Night at the Movies* was playing. I loved watching *Saturday Night at the Movies* because it meant staying up an hour past my bedtime. Aunt Louise leaned back in her chair, resting her feet on the ottoman. As the opening credits rolled, Clem pulled me next to him and rubbed my head with his big, rough hands. For the rest of the evening he seemed in a better mood.

When it was time for bed, Clem put on his long underwear and slipped under the army blanket. Louise and I slept in her double bed in the back bedroom, the same bedroom where Clem had fallen from a ladder, breaking his ankle so badly it never healed properly. Louise put on a nightdress and let down her long gray hair, which made her look like a large, wrinkled child. We knelt beside the bed and said the Lord's Prayer. We crawled into bed and slept with our backs against each other.

On the mantel over the gas stove ticked a clock Louise and Clem's father had brought back from a trip to Philadelphia around the turn of the century. I loved to run my fingers along its polished black surface and over the lion faces on either side. Sometimes I lifted the clock down and opened the tin backing to examine its inner workings. I was intrigued with the idea that the heavy swinging pendulum and the slowly revolving cogwheels translated themselves into minutes and hours. Sometimes I lifted out the pendulum, silencing the clock. I was God as I hefted the cold lead weight in the palm of my hand; time was mine to stop.

The clock ticked loudly; usually the sound lulled me to sleep, but tonight I stared at the ceiling. My mother was having a baby.

"Where do people go when they die?" I asked Aunt Louise.

A train whistled, its cars rattling over the tracks that ran on the edge of Colored Town. Mitchell and I used to line pennies along the rail.

Louise took so long to answer that I thought she had fallen asleep. "To the hereafter," she finally said, yawning. The stove clicked and then whooshed on, filling the room with warmth and light.

"What do you have to do to get there?" I asked, staring at the square of blue flames.

"Believe," she said, her voice far away.

"Believe what?"

My aunt was asleep, breathing steadily beside me. And when, in a while, the stove cut off, the clock was my only company.

THE NEXT MORNING, LOUISE WOKE EARLY to help Clem with his ankle. I sat on his cot as he, still in his long johns, unwrapped the Ace bandage. Louise removed the brown swatch of gauze, revealing a crusty wound. A sour smell filled the den. She let me pour the hydrogen peroxide, then she cleaned the spot, replaced the gauze, rewrapped the bandage, and pinned it. She had done this every morning for four years, since his fall.

After breakfast, Louise and I dressed for church and went for our Sunday-morning walk. Their house was in a row of what had been well-kept homes across from the old Furman University campus. Some of the houses had belonged to faculty or had been used to board students. But, like theirs, most had begun to show neglect. "For Sale" signs had sprung up, but no one wanted homes with an abandoned campus on one side and Colored Town on the other.

Louise and I walked along the broken sidewalk that connected the old brick classroom buildings to the bell tower. Its chimes had stopped sounding the hours, leaving the neighborhood without a timekeeper.

Louise leaned against me for support, pressing the ground with her cane. We had made this trek from the time I could walk. The three of us would walk up the sidewalk—me, the overweight too-blond boy, on one side of Aunt Louise, and Mitchell, the dark, lean one, on the other.

We passed the ivy-covered administration building, where Louise had worked. When I was four years old, the college, a men's school, had merged with Greenville's women's college and moved outside of town. We passed the old auditorium where Aunt Louise had heard Thomas Edison speak and then had actually shaken his hand. "What did he say?" I would ask. "He said, 'Nice to meet you,' " Aunt Louise would reply. Maybe that was all he had said, but I knew he had wanted to ask her to lunch. He had wanted to go to a movie with her. If Thomas Edison so much as shook my aunt's hand, he would have wanted to marry her.

I knew this wasn't all that far-fetched. Over the course of Aunt Louise's life she had had a number of proposals, but when Aunt Louise's sister—my great-grandmother— died, then Aunt Louise had felt responsible for mothering her sister's four children, Grandma Grace among them. This had also been true when Grandma Grace died, leaving my mother and Uncle Charlie. My mother said that Aunt Louise had been too busy raising everyone else's children to marry or have children of her own.

We stopped to rest where we usually stopped—underneath a bronze statue of a doughboy, a monument to the Furman men who had died in World War I. I climbed onto the statue, my head even with the rifle.

Louise sat on the cement bench, leaning on her cane and looking away from the buildings and out over what I thought of as the real campus—a wooded oval of land about the size of two city blocks with an open field in the middle. It was crisscrossed by dirt paths, worn by decades of students and professors walking between home and school. Now the only people to traverse the campus were those from the neighborhood on their way to the Eight O'Clock Superette or Baker's Laundromat or out for a stroll. And then there were boys like me and Mitchell, who had spent long afternoons throwing a baseball in the field or sitting and listening to the wind whisper through the pines.

A familiar Negro man crossed the old campus. He was dressed in his Sunday clothes and a small dog trotted beside him, the same little dog that had been chained up across the creek. The man touched the bill of his hat as he approached. "Miss Louise."

"Blakely," Aunt Louise raised her hand.

He nodded at me. "Mister Jeru."

Without a word, I dropped down from the statue and sat beside my aunt. He walked on across the field, the little dog running ahead. I watched until they were out of sight.

After Mitchell had been killed, a tremor of shock and then outrage shook the neighborhood, spilling into other parts of the city. After all, this wasn't just an accident between neighbors; a Negro's dog had killed a white child. There was an outcry against Colored Town—the Greenville *Piedmont* published dozens of enraged letters to the editor and, according to my mother, received hundreds more. For weeks, a general distrust took hold of neighborhoods, as parents worried about the hazards of dogs and their children playing in the streets. Mr. Blakely received more than a couple of threats on his life.

In the midst of all this, my mother, on her return to work, wrote "A Letter to Greenville," in which she said that Mr. Blakely had not been at fault and neither had the dog (an important point to her). She wrote that "the community should not allow a tragic accident to drive some of us to blame the blameless."

The rest of my family was too lost in grief to consider

anything as deliberate as forgiveness. However, they were so relieved to have my mother out of her bedroom and back in the world that when she asked my father and Aunt Louise to sign her letter, they did so without hesitation. Uncle Clem, on the other hand, flatly refused.

The paper was reluctant to publish my mother's letter, which couldn't have been more counter to public sentiment. It was a testament to just how respected my mother was as a journalist that they finally did run the letter. Time and the letter seemed to defuse much of the hostility. If the child's own mother didn't want retribution, the townspeople seemed to think, then maybe they should let it go as well. Within a few months, my brother's death had lost its public resonance and settled into our own private loss.

WHEN WE RETURNED FROM OUR WALK, we heard gunshots. Aunt Louise and Uncle Clem's next-door neighbor Mary Moore was standing in her front yard in her night robe. "He's at it again. I know they're pests, but does he have to shoot them on Sunday morning?"

"I'll take care of it," Aunt Louise said, and we walked to the back and found Clem in his Sunday clothes, aiming his rifle at the roof. A pigeon stuck its head out. Clem fired. Nothing happened. The sound of the shot echoed off the houses. I thought he had missed until the bird toppled into the gutter, fluttered against the house, then plopped, lifeless, onto the grass beside the goldfish pond.

"You got him!" I ran over, picked up the still warm bird, and brought it to Clem.

"Little Brother!" Louise shook her cane at him. "It's Sunday morning. Mary is about to call the police."

Clem twisted the bird's neck. "I was passing the time till

y'all got back." He laid it on top of a big barrel with two other pigeons. Later, he would pluck and clean them for his supper. They would emerge from the oven, browned miniature chickens. While neighbors and relatives, including my parents, had warned him that pigeons spread disease and could be dangerous to eat, this did not curb my uncle's appetite for the birds on his roof.

Putting his gun inside the shop door, he limped around to the garage and backed out the Model A, which they drove mostly to the Eight O'Clock Superette and church. I helped Louise into her seat, then hopped into the back. The car smelled of leather and oil. Clem backed us out into the street, ground it into gear, and pressed the gas.

We rattled down Howe Street toward Pendleton Street Baptist Church, where, probably for the first time, I did not squirm in the hard pew or cover my ears from the preacher's harangues but sat transfixed by the stained-glass window of Mary holding the baby Jesus. Her face commanded my attention. She wore such a serene expression, not like a mother smiling adoringly upon her newborn, but like a woman who already understood what would have to happen.

CHAPTER THREE

A Safe Place

News of my mother's pregnancy sent tremors through our household. My father took it hard, believing my mother had deceived him into having another baby. She thought of it as divine intervention—the miraculous result of her newly found faith. Deliberately or not, though, she had made him an unwilling accomplice in creating a new life and endangering her own. Confrontation was not in my father's nature, but simmering was.

It wasn't until nearly a month later that I heard him address the subject and then only after my mother had brought it up. We were on one of our Sunday-afternoon drives, one my father hadn't wanted to go on in the first place. Ever since he had found out about the pregnancy, he had spent most of his time in his office, typing furiously. But my mother, who seemed to have a renewed sense of family, went down to his office one afternoon and led him by the arm out to the car. We piled into the Chevrolet and drove into the mountains to view the foliage.

As we left Greenville behind, I fingered a blue letter in my pant pocket. The day before, I had been outside when the mailman brought the mail, which, as I carried it into the house, I noticed contained another blue letter. Since it was Saturday, my mother was at home making lunch. With my father in the basement, I knew my mother would see the mail first. I slipped the letter into my pocket, thinking that was what my father would have wanted, and I set the rest of the mail on the foyer table.

But I couldn't just present him with the blue letter or he would know I had noticed. I worried half the afternoon until I realized I could slip the letter into Monday's stack of mail. I felt as charged with its safekeeping as if the Hope diamond had come into my possession.

We were halfway up a steep mountain called Caesar's Head, our old car bucking, when my mother asked my father when he planned to return to the ad agency, what with the baby imminent. My father didn't reply but shifted roughly into a lower gear, making the engine whine. He angrily tapped a cigarette from the pack in his shirt pocket, lit it with the car lighter, and with one hand steered around a sharp curve that opened onto a long view of the valley below.

My mother calmly watched a roadside shower of October leaves that tapped across the hood and wedged behind the windshield wipers.

"I knew this was coming," my father said finally, glancing into the rearview mirror at the lengthening trail of cars. He shifted into second. The engine whined louder. "I can't go back to writing slogans for toilet-bowl cleaners and laundry detergents. I can't operate on that plane anymore."

"As long as we live on this plane, we have to pay the bills on this plane," she said, pulling her sweater over her shoulders. "The society section is no picnic. Sometimes I think if I have to describe one more wedding gown or print one more turkey tetrazzini recipe . . ." She sighed. "But I do because it helps make ends meet."

He flicked his cigarette into the ashtray. "Early man devoted three hours a day to hunting food. The rest of his day was spent relaxing and roaming the woods."

"I would be happy for you to write all day," my mother said, "but the truth is that we're running out of time."

"How could you?" My father slammed his palm on the steering wheel. "How could you do this to us?"

My mother sat calmly and watched the road. My father muttered something else and took a long drag from his cigarette.

"When does the baby get here?" Henry asked.

"It's not coming by bus," I said from behind my book.

"In February." My mother reached back and touched Henry's head. He sat with me in the backseat, holding his hand out the window. I had been reading a little book I had found in the school library called *Hiroshima,* about six survivors of the atom bomb.

I turned a page of the first chapter, entitled "A Noiseless Flash," but my mind was on my father. I had never seen him so distraught. I hadn't expected it. He was the one who had coped when Mitchell was killed. He had seen to the funeral arrangements, cooked meals, put us to bed, seen me off to school each morning. I fingered the letter again. I had slept with it under my pillow. I had tried not to think about opening it.

Our car crawled up the steep switchback. Caesar's Head had a sheer rock face that rose out of the piedmont, signaling the beginning of the Blue Ridge Mountains. I hated that the afternoon was unraveling. I cherished Sunday-afternoon rides into the mountains, especially after mornings spent at church.

Earlier, my mother had taken Henry and me with her to the Christian Science church, which she attended almost every Sunday morning. My father never went. But my mother had gone since the day she had emerged from the bedroom, and she took us with her—another reason I preferred staying with Aunt Louise and Uncle Clem on the weekends; I felt much more at home in their little Baptist church, where we went in, sang hymns, had the preacher yell at us, sang more hymns, and then left. But at the Church of Christ, Scientist, as the stylish wooden sign out front read, my mother attended the adult service, leaving Henry and me to Sunday-school classes taught by well-meaning but overly serious Northerners, who talked about Divine Science in such long words and complicated sentences that I left feeling it wasn't faith I needed but a dictionary.

We continued on up Caesar's Head. I closed my book and stared out the window at a hawk floating over the valley. Forty miles behind us lay Greenville, along the banks of the Reedy River. Besides its mills, Greenville's other claim to fame was its drinking water, which was piped in from a pristine reservoir in the mountainous northern edge of the county. Next to some hamlet in Switzerland, ours was the purest in the world, a fact the Chamber of Commerce posted on every welcome sign. It wasn't exactly an attraction; tourists didn't flock to our city to try the water. But when Greenvillians traveled, all it took was a sip of the local water to remind us of home.

I stared out the rear windshield and saw Greenville in the distance, a collection of miniature buildings, a blocky interruption in the rolling hills. There was a flash, a distant rumble. The ground shook. The mountain trembled. A mushroom cloud curled up into the sky, lifting my town on a firestorm of billowing radiation. Donaldson Elementary, the Lewis Plaza Pharmacy, Mackey's Funeral Home, the Sanitary Bakery, Dr. Norton's office, the old Furman campus, Cleveland Park, and the houses of Afton Avenue all rode the boiling clouds high into the stratosphere. I blinked. The mushroom cloud vanished. Greenville resumed its tentative place on the horizon.

I felt in my other pocket for Mitchell's arrowhead, holding it in my palm. Mitchell had found it the day before he was killed. He had come out back to help with the weeding. He had only been hoeing for five minutes when he found it in the roots of a clump of chickweed. I had an Indian collection at home—fragments of what I hoped might be arrowheads and bits of pottery, but nothing in my collection was as whole or as flawless as what Mitchell held in his hand. He showed it to Uncle Clem, who polished it on his shirtsleeve then handed it to me. It was made of beautiful white flint. I poked the pointed tip with my finger.

"Come on. Give it back." Mitchell impatiently held out his hand.

Later that afternoon, I saw it drop from his shirt pocket when he leaned over. We hoed together the rest of the afternoon, the arrowhead burning a hole in my pocket. I never told him. A day later, he was dead.

We passed roadside stands crowded with tourists buying honey, cider, and bags of Winesap, Gala, or Golden Delicious apples. In a month, these same stands would be boarded up.

"Pull over." My mother pointed to an apple stand. "I want to take a couple of bagfuls to the newsroom."

Ignoring her, my father kept driving, smoking his cigarette to the butt. The thermometer on the dashboard edged toward "H." Wisps of steam curled around the hood. We reached the crest. The parking lot to the lookout tower overflowed with sightseers. We started down the other side, which didn't have so much traffic. Most everyone came from the direction of Greenville. There were no stands on this side of the mountain, and there were long stretches of uninterrupted woods. Water trickled down the rocks, making small waterfalls along the roadside.

"There's Walden." Henry tapped on the window at a half-hidden cabin, set back from the road with a little pond. My father had started the idea a few years before when he said he bet Thoreau could have been happy there. We didn't know who Thoreau was except that our father thought a lot of him. Over the years it became our dream cabin. But that afternoon my father didn't so much as glance in its direction.

The car began an all-too-familiar chug and shudder and then cut off. We coasted into a clearing beside the road that had a couple of picnic tables. The four of us sat in the car, something hissing under the hood. A few cars passed.

My father gripped the steering wheel, his knuckles white. "I can't go through this." He stared straight ahead.

"This baby is a gift." My mother started to take his hand.

He slammed his fist onto the dashboard.

"It will be all right," my mother said, putting her hand on his shoulder. "I know it will."

He groaned, rolling his forehead against the steering wheel, talking into his lap. "You didn't really see him."

"Don't, Warren." Her eyes reddened.

He looked at her. "You didn't ride in the ambulance."

She pressed her hands over her ears.

He pulled her hands down. "You didn't see his face."

"Stop it," she said, trying to pull her hands away. "Not in front of the children."

He let go of her hands. "I'm sorry." He leaned over as if to hug her, but then he jumped out of the car and opened the hood with his handkerchief. A geyser of steam rose up, enveloping the car. My father shouted something. The steam began to clear, but we couldn't see him behind the open hood.

My mother leaned out her window. "How does it look?"

No answer. Cars passed on the road. A breeze blew through the open window. Leaves showered down upon the car. Autumn was much further along up here. The air was so much cooler. This was a lighter, less encumbered atmosphere.

"Warren?" My mother opened her door, looking back at us. "Stay in the car."

Henry and I waited in the backseat. The hood blocked our view. Cars kept passing.

"He's gone." Our mother stuck her head in our window. "It's chilly out here."

Henry and I pulled on our sweaters as we ran around to the front of the car. Steam still boiled from the radiator. There was no sign of our father, except for his handkerchief lying on the ground beside the radiator cap.

"Maybe he went to pee." Henry looked toward a small path leading into the woods.

My mother leaned over the open hood. "A broken hose."

Henry and I followed her to the trunk, which she

opened with the keys my father had left in the ignition. "He must have taken out the toolbox," she said, shaking her head. She looked under a bag of old shoes. "Not even a screwdriver." She sighed. "We'll have to sit and wait for him." She went over and sat on one of the picnic-table benches set in the clearing. Henry sat beside her.

Feeling like the man in charge, I walked over to the path, taking a couple of steps into the woods. The beginning of the path was littered with crushed beer cans and candy wrappers. I took a few steps down the path. Fallen limbs lay all around me as I breathed in the dark smell of moldering leaves. I stood at the top of a switchback trail that led down the mountainside. He hadn't gone to pee. Henry knew that. My mother knew that.

I cupped my hands to my mouth. "Da-deeee!"

I walked back to the front of the car, where a little steam still puffed out of the radiator. I picked up my father's handkerchief.

"Any sign of him?" my mother asked.

I handed her the handkerchief and sat beside them at the picnic table.

It wasn't long before an old station wagon pulled up. A man got out and came over to us. He was dressed in a coat too short in the sleeves and wore a bright pink tie. His wife waited in the station wagon with about half a dozen children squeezed into the back. They were dressed in church clothes.

"Need a hand?" he asked in a thick mountain accent.

"My husband should return any minute." My mother glanced in the direction of the woods. "I think."

"You think?" The man took off his cap and scratched his head.

"Our car overheated, he opened the hood, and then he vanished." My mother gave a nervous laugh.

The man studied us, then the woods. He must have been about my father's age, but he had the lean, hollow-eyed look of a man who makes his living from physical labor. Maybe a farmer or a carpenter or a mechanic. His hands were big and calloused. He looked uncomfortable in his Sunday clothes.

"Where could Daddy have gone?" my mother asked me.

I shrugged.

"Maybe he went for help," the man said. "I'll take a peak under the hood."

"I think a water hose is broken," my mother said.

We all followed the man to our car, watching as he bent over the engine, checking wires and lifting hoses.

"You was right, ma'am." The man turned to my mother, new respect in his tone. "Let me get my tools."

He opened the back of his station wagon, unleashing a whirlwind of children that ran circles around us, finally gathering around our car.

"Don't y'all get your good clothes dirty 'fore we even get to the church." The mother came up behind them. She was a plain woman with eyes as blue as Aunt Louise's teacups. She wore a stiff yellow dress and high heels that wobbled when she walked. "Lester," she said to her husband, "leastways take off your coat and tie."

The man let her slip off his coat and unknot his tie. She folded them carefully and set them on one of the picnic tables.

"I'm sorry to interrupt your Sunday-afternoon church," my mother said to the woman.

"We was on our way to a wedding."

"Won't you be late?"

"We left early." The woman tugged at her dress sleeve. "Besides, it's somebody on Lester's side and they's barely kin. Cousin of a cousin of a cousin. Hardly anybody." She nodded to her husband, who had an audience now. "Lester'd rather be under a hood than under a steeple any day." She sat on the picnic table, and my mother sat with her. "Did I hear you say your husband left?"

My mother looked toward the woods again. "One minute he was here. The next minute he was gone."

The woman tucked her dress between her legs.

Henry rested his head in our mother's lap. "My mama is having a baby," he said to the woman.

"Henry." My mother pulled him against her. "We don't have to broadcast it."

The woman lowered her eyes to my mother's stomach. "You ain't far along."

"Five months."

"Least you'll have it before summer."

"My daddy got mad and the car got hot," Henry said to the woman. "So here we are."

The woman went over to the station wagon and came back with a pound cake wrapped in wax paper and a kitchen knife. She removed the wax paper and began to cut pieces. She handed a piece to my mother, one to Henry, and one to me. I wolfed down my piece; it was moist and buttery, even better than the Sanitary Bakery.

"Was this for the wedding?" My mother bit into the cake.

"Yes," said the woman, "but this is an emergency." She cut pieces for all the children as they swarmed around. She took a piece to her husband, then sat beside my mother, cutting one for herself. "Your husband will come back soon." She brushed a crumb from my mother's sweater.

All the color had drained out of my mother's face. I fingered the letter in my pocket. The more desperate and worried my mother became, the more I believed I should do something. I wondered if perhaps there was something in the letter that might tell us where he had gone.

The man finished patching the water hose with duct tape, then he took some empty milk bottles out of the back of his station wagon, handed a couple to his oldest boy, and the two of them walked down the road to where water trickled down a mossy rock. I watched, envious that the son had a father who kept a toolbox in his car and knew what to do with it.

Finally, I stepped into the woods and, making sure I was out of sight, pulled the envelope from my pocket. Telling myself it was my duty to find out where my father had gone, I opened my knife and neatly slit the envelope. I slipped out the blue piece of paper and, looking around again to make sure I was alone, unfolded it.

I remember a profound sense of disappointment when I saw that it was only a letter, only words written in the same shaky handwriting that I had seen on the letters in my father's office. I don't know what I had been hoping for. Perhaps a diagram or a map with clues that would need decoding and a big *X* marking the spot where treasure was buried. Even after I had read the letter, I still felt let down. It was only on the second and third readings that I began to get a faint inkling of what it said.

The letter was only a few sentences long, and while I cannot remember it word for word, I do remember it was signed by a woman named Sarah who said she was sorry about Mitchell's death, but that she could not tell my father where "Caroline and the girl" had moved. I do remember the sentence "They would not want anything to do with you, even if they happened to live next door." The other sentence I remember is "And, no, I cannot tell you the child's name." The letter ended by asking my father not to write again.

As I stood there, reading the letter over, the words began to float on the page, as if on the surface of a well I was looking into, a well I hadn't even known existed. I don't know how many times my mother had called me before I heard her. I stuffed the letter in one pocket and the envelope in the other pocket and hurried out of the woods.

"Oh, thank goodness," my mother said, hugging me as I came into the clearing, "I thought we had lost you, too." She led me to the picnic table where Henry and the woman still sat. I was aware that the other children were playing freeze tag along the edge of the woods, that traffic had begun to die down, and that the air had cooled, but my mind was still deciphering what I had read. Who was my father looking for? Had he left us to try and find them?

"What should I do?" My mother paced in front of the picnic tables. She ran her hand through her thick hair. "Should I call the police? The forest ranger? I don't even know which way he went."

I watched one of the children, a girl with pigtails. She looked about my age. She had dirty-blond hair and her mother's blue eyes. She reminded me of Norma Jones. She ran faster than any of the others and when she was "it" she froze everybody before they ran ten feet. These could have been Norma's relatives, the same people who lived on the other side of Augusta Road, except these people lived on the other side of the mountain. The same people my mother meant when she scolded me for tracing my finger on our dusty windshield, because we might be mistaken for the kind of people who didn't know better.

When the man and his son returned, the man asked my mother to start the car, then he began filling the radiator with water from the bottles. When he finished, he replaced the radiator cap and checked under the hood.

"That ought to hold you till you can get down the mountain." The man wiped his greasy hands on a handkerchief.

My mother fished her wallet from her pocketbook and tried to hand him a five-dollar bill, but the man closed my mother's hand over the money.

"What's she going to do about her husband?" the woman asked.

He scratched his head and studied us, as if considering whether he had room at his house for three more. I remember wishing he did. I wanted to go home with this man and his buoyant family, so sure of themselves, so prepared for whatever befell them.

"If we just had a clue which way he went," my mother said.

I felt the envelope in my pocket. Deciding not to give everything away at once, I handed the empty envelope to my mother, saying, "I found this down one of the paths."

My mother turned the opened envelope over in her hands. "It's addressed to Warren. And the return address is Wilmington." My mother looked at me. "Why didn't you say something about this sooner?"

"I have a cousin in Wilmington." The woman looked over my mother's shoulder. "That ain't his handwriting. That's a woman's handwriting."

My mother looked inside the envelope. "Did you see anything else over there?" She slid the envelope into her pocketbook.

"That's all." I kept my hand in my pocket, feeling the letter itself.

A horn sounded, and a wrecker pulled off the highway and backed next to our car. The driver hopped out, then my father. He directed the driver, a man with a handlebar mustache, over to our car.

"We've been worried sick." My mother gestured to include the mother and the children and the father.

"I hitched a ride," my father said. "Didn't you see me wave?"

"Lester Perkins." The man shook my father's hand vigorously. "Glad you come back."

The woman dusted herself off and took my father's hand. "You done the right thing."

"They have missed a wedding to help us," my mother said.

My father pulled his wallet out. "What do I owe you?"

"Missing a wedding is payment enough," Mr. Perkins said. He and the wrecker driver consulted under the hood, while my father explained to my mother how he had caught a ride with a couple and ridden around until he found an open gas station.

The children played tag all through this. The blond girl ran over to me. "All you do is watch." She tagged me hard on the shoulder. "You're 'it.' " I chased her as fast as I could, but she knew how to run just fast enough to stay out of reach.

After the Perkinses had left, we started down the mountain. My father sat back in his seat, driving with one hand.

Ever since he had returned with the wrecker, he hadn't seemed as tense.

After a little while my mother rested her hand on his shoulder. "I never meant to deceive you," she said.

My father took a drag on his cigarette. I watched Henry looking out the car window. His profile was so much like Mitchell's. I couldn't help reaching over and touching his arm.

He turned. "What?"

I didn't say anything. I picked up my book, holding it at an angle to catch the last light. When the bomb went off over Hiroshima, a clerk was sitting down to her desk, a doctor was about to read the morning paper, a housewife was standing at her kitchen sink looking out the window.

"So you don't want the baby?" my mother asked my father.

"I wouldn't say that," my father said in a faraway voice.

"You do want the baby?"

"I wouldn't say that either." My father set the cigarette in the ashtray, filling the car with sweet smoke, a smell that made me feel safe.

I closed the book. We passed by the empty parking lot of the observation tower and the apple stands, the sides of which were now closed up tight. We joined a long line of traffic snaking down the mountain.

"Who lives in Wilmington?" my mother asked, as she pulled the blue envelope out of her purse.

"Where did you find that?" My father looked at the envelope.

"Jeru found it." My mother yawned and laid her head on the seat. "There's nothing in it."

I felt my father glance at me in the rearview mirror. "It's

from a mother of an old friend I have been trying to track down. Somebody I knew when I worked for the Cotton Council."

The tires screeched out of the curves. On one side was the mountain wall, on the other, night sky. Greenville glowed in the distance.

"Were you able to get his address?" She closed her eyes.

"*Her* address," he said, a little quieter.

My mother opened her eyes. "You're trying to track down an old girlfriend?"

"A book of an old girlfriend. I lent her my *Walden.*"

"You're tracking down a book that you already have at least three copies of?"

"It was my grandfather's."

I opened my book, but it was too dark to read, so I made up my own story. Jeru Lamb and his family were returning from a Sunday drive in the mountains when the atom bomb was dropped on Greenville, South Carolina. As they drove toward what had been their city, they found in its place a scorched absence.

Henry rolled up his window to keep out the chilly night air. He pressed his hand against the glass and said, indicating the night sky, "The moon keeps up with us."

"CAN I BORROW A PEN?" I ASKED my father as I sized up the connect-the-dots drawing on the children's place mat. My mother and Henry had gone to the bathrooms.

"Pronounced *pen.*" My father handed me one of his pens from his coat pocket, clicking it open.

"Pen," I repeated, feeling my mouth seize up.

My father watched me while I connected the dots of a drawing of Simple Simon and the Pie Man. He took another pen out of his pocket, turned over his mat, and began to sketch an oval that would become a woman's face.

We had stopped to eat supper at Howard Johnson, which always felt opulent with its polished tables, its shiny tile floors, and its laminated menus. Even the food had a sheen. But it was the desserts that transformed us—elaborate sundaes with twenty-eight flavors of ice cream and almost as many sauces, fudge cakes awash in chocolate icing, rich pies piled high with whipped cream. My family was never more animated than when we ate dessert in our booth at Howard Johnson. It was as social as we got, eating in a restaurant full of other people eating.

Still sketching, my father leaned across the table, speaking in a low voice. "When you found the envelope, did you find anything else?"

I didn't look up but started on another connect-the-dots drawing of a banana split.

"Where did you get that letter?"

My pen slipped and cut across the place mat.

The waitress hurried to our table with four glasses of water. She was a pretty woman in her late twenties. She wore the orange Howard Johnson uniform. She touched my father's hand. "Thanks for recommending *Brothers Karamazov*." She took out her pad. "I didn't know Dostoevsky was epileptic."

"You might try *The Idiot* next." My father put out his cigarette in the ashtray. "It's a little less generous but much more profound."

"*The Idiot*." She turned her pad over and scribbled the title on the back. "I'll go ahead and get your drinks—two Cokes and two coffees."

My father waited until she was out of earshot and then

leaned across the table. "It's wrong to read other people's mail." He took a drag on his cigarette, sliding the ashtray over in front of him. "What did you do with it?" He grabbed my arm but then let go when my mother came out of the bathroom.

"Slide over, honey," she said to my father.

I saw Henry come out of the men's bathroom and jumped up. I started across the restaurant and slipped into the bathroom, but the door wouldn't lock, so I ran into the stall and locked the door. As I took the letter out of my pocket, I heard the bathroom door open.

My father's shoes appeared at the bottom of the stall. He rattled the door. In my panic I balled up the piece of paper, dropped it into the commode and flushed it. Then I opened the stall door. He was standing there, his cigarette hanging out of the side of his mouth. He looked at me, then he looked at the commode. He tossed his cigarette into the water, making a fizzle.

"I didn't mean to open the letter," I said. "I took it from the mail so Mama wouldn't see it."

He still stared at the commode. "At least tell me what it said."

"It said she won't tell you where they are, whoever it is you're looking for."

My father sighed. "Was worth a try," he said to himself, then he looked up at me. "Jeru, this was something that happened before your mother. A detour on my way to us, our family." He went to the urinal, unzipped his pants, and peed, talking to me over his shoulder. "You're too young." He zipped his pants and went to the sink to wash his hands. "You won't understand all that I'm telling you."

He pulled out a clean section of the cloth towel, drying his hands.

"The lousy thing was that she was a couple of months pregnant when I met your mother, and one thing led to another . . ." He put his hand on my cheek. "It led to you." His eyes were bloodshot. "Even if you don't understand now, you will some day. And you're the only one who, maybe not now, but in ten or twenty years, might be in a position to forgive me." He draped his arm over my shoulder. "I'm asking if what was in that letter can be kept just between us?"

I looked into my father's beseeching eyes and nodded.

He clapped me on the back. He was relieved, and I felt heartened, more responsible, more grown-up, more of a man now that I shared his secret. Whatever it was.

THE WAITRESS HAD FINISHED SERVING our desserts when she looked out the window. Her smile faded. A new Cadillac had pulled to the curb and a well-dressed Negro couple with a little girl and a little boy got out and started into the restaurant.

"Michigan license plates," my father said, taking a spoonful of sherbet.

"They're coming in," my mother said.

Sighing to herself, the waitress headed off to the corner to clear a table.

Before the family reached the foyer, the manager was out the door, meeting them on the sidewalk, his arms crossed. The Negro man said something. The manager shook his head. The Negro man said something else, frowning. The manager unfolded his arms and shook his head again. For a minute no one moved. The boy and the girl looked through the window at Henry and me, it seemed.

"What's the man saying?" Henry asked.

"He's telling them that they can't come in," my father said.

I didn't have to ask my father why they couldn't come in. I already knew. We lived in a cleanly divided world, and it had not occurred to me that anyone would want it any other way.

"How dare they," said a woman in the booth behind us, a mother sitting across from two older girls, all in Sunday clothes. An uncomfortable silence had descended on the restaurant, with everyone staring out the window.

The Negro woman said something to the manager. She moved her arms wildly, shaking her finger in his face and shouting loud enough so that we could faintly hear her voice, if not her words, causing the window to vibrate. Her husband took her arm and began to lead her back to the car. As they got in the car, the boy, wearing a coat and tie like his father's, turned around and stared in my direction as I took a big bite of my sundae.

The manager stayed out front with his arms folded and watched them get in the car. The noise in the restaurant resumed as people returned to their meals.

"They probably thought this was a safe place since Howard Johnson is a chain . . ." My mother pushed her fudge cake to the middle of the table. "Shouldn't we do something?" She looked at my father, who had stopped eating too.

"Like what? Enlighten a restaurant full of bigots?" He

said it loudly enough so that the woman behind us stiff-ened.

"We could complain to the manager," my mother said. "Tell him we'll never eat here again." But as soon as she said it, we all knew it wasn't true.

As the car pulled away, the manager strode back in and returned to his chair behind the cash register, his face flushed in triumph.

In a little while, the waitress returned to refill our water glasses. She was smiling at us, but when she spoke her tone was flat. "Do y'all want anything else? More coffee?" she asked, tearing the ticket off her pad and setting it on the table.

I ate my sundae greedily, trying to savor every bite. Even though the family was gone, I did not dare look out the window, afraid I would see that boy still there, want-ing something of mine.

CHAPTER FOUR

The Reedy River

NOVEMBER WAS A QUIET MONTH AT HOME, but the quiet, in truth, was only a lull. My mother's morning sickness had abated, replaced by an almost daily craving for a hot dog all the way from Pete's Drive-In that even Divine Principle could not assuage. My father seemed calmer, as if resigned to the coming baby. He also had more time for Henry and me. After supper, he tossed the football with us outside or played Monopoly or Careers on the den floor. But sometimes, in the middle of a game, his eyes would glaze over, his mind obviously gone somewhere else. In a way, he was more absent when he was with us than when he closed himself up in his office and typed.

Roger Avant and I spent a good bit of time together. I doubt that either of us thought of it as need that was bringing us together, but that is exactly what it was—a need for another boy.

We often rode our bikes the three blocks to the McDaniel Heights apartments, where his father had moved. Lately, we had been testing an elaborate box kite Roger and Dr. Avant had designed for the Indian Guides competition. Indian Guides was a YMCA organization for fathers and sons. Roger and Dr. Avant not only built things and wore Indian headbands, they went on camping trips together. I envied this. My father was not an outdoorsman. For him, nature was a scenic overlook, a distant panorama viewed through a ticking telescope that went black when our quarter was up.

Roger and I usually spent the afternoon in the big field behind his father's apartment building, racing the kite back and forth trying to get it airborne, while Dr. Avant made adjustments. I didn't like going inside. The McDaniel Heights apartments were painted the same deadening green as Donaldson's classrooms, and the halls breathed a stale, lonely smell. I didn't like being in the same room with Dr. Avant, fearing that he might diagnose me. Also, he pronounced my name with the accent on the last syllable, like a birdcall. "Je-ruuu."

Roger bicycled with his brothers all over town, and he knew outlying neighborhoods, the world beyond. One chilly afternoon on our way home from his father's apartment, he asked if I wanted to see where Miss Hawkins lived. Without waiting for a reply, he turned onto an unfamiliar street. I had to pedal hard to keep up. Rusted and fenderless, Roger's bike, like most of his things, had belonged to his brothers. The years had stripped it of everything except speed. Roger rode his bike like a jockey rides a horse, crouched against the wind, his bottom in the air. He bounced on his knees, anticipating every bump, every turn, every last-second swerve.

Eventually, Roger skidded to a stop in front of a small, bright clapboard house with white shutters and a picket fence—a far cry from the looming, dark house I had imagined. A small dog lay in a pool of sunlight in the middle of the raked yard. A Siamese blinked at us from an upstairs window.

"This is it." Roger straddled his bike, resting his arms on the handlebars.

"She has pets," I whispered, unzipping my windbreaker and trying to catch my breath.

"Let's look in the window," he said.

"What if she's there?"

"Her car's not in the driveway." We hid our bikes behind a large azalea bush. The dog lifted his head, sniffed the air, and then lowered his head. We slipped behind the hedge, and, as we did, a curtain moved. We froze. The Siamese had moved in the window, wanting a closer look.

Miss Hawkins had seemed less dangerous now that we had survived two months in her class. We had, in fact, learned a great deal: parts of speech, long division, the capitals of all fifty states. Still, the possibility of being caught made my heart race, but Roger, who was usually very cautious concerning Miss Hawkins, seemed almost cavalier.

We crept to the back of the house and squinted through the kitchen window. It appeared to be a regular kitchen with flour and sugar canisters on the counter, potholders on a hook by the stove, a can opener attached to the wall next to the sink.

Roger and I pressed our noses against the window. We must have pressed a little too hard because the door swung open. We hesitated, smelling something simmering in a big pot on the stove. I started to close the door, but Roger put his foot against it. "She's not here," he said, raising his eyebrows.

"What if she comes home?" I whispered.

"We'll hear her." Roger stepped into the kitchen, looked around, then took a couple of more steps. I followed him.

He lifted the lid of the big pot.

We looked in.

"Chicken soup." He looked at me.

I nodded.

We went through all the kitchen cabinets. "She likes Jif." Roger held up a jar of peanut butter.

I opened the refrigerator. There was a jar of sweet pickles, a half-full serving dish of congealed fruit salad, and a pan of fudge with only a few pieces left. I lifted the wax paper and picked up a square of fudge.

"What are you doing?" Roger stared at me.

I held the pan of fudge out to him. He lifted a piece out and bit into it. Licking our fingers, we tiptoed through the rest of the house, which smelled like the inside of a cedar chest. I picked up a framed photograph on the mantel. It was of a man and a woman and a girl in pigtails posed stiffly in front of a small white house. "That looks like a Mill's Mill house."

Roger came over. "It is." He indicated the water tower in the background.

"And who is that girl?"

"Miss Hawkins," Roger said.

We heard the slam of a car door outside. Through the window, we saw Miss Hawkins marching up her walk with a bag of groceries. I placed the picture on the mantel, but it slipped and broke on the floor. I started to pick up the pieces, but Roger grabbed my shirt. We raced through the kitchen and heard the front door open as Roger quietly closed the back door. We raced through the backyard, down a brick path, and around the side of the yard, keeping low among the hedges. This time the dog barked. We rolled our bikes out of the bushes, jumped on, and pedaled for all we were worth.

Mrs. Roberts, the school librarian, looked up from her house across the street. She was raking leaves. Even after we turned the corner, I still felt her eyes on us. We didn't stop to catch our breath until we reached Pine Forest Drive.

Finally, we turned and looked back down the road. Roger wasn't as winded as I was.

"I should tell her I broke her picture," I panted.

"She'll know we were walking around inside her house," said Roger, sitting back on his bike.

"We were," I said.

"You think you're George Washington or somebody." Roger leaned over his handlebars. "You want to know how come he really chopped down the cherry tree?"

"How come?"

"So he could look good when he told on himself," he said. "You're the same way."

Furious, I turned my bike around and started pedaling toward Miss Hawkins's.

"Where are you going?"

I was too angry to speak. I kept pedaling. It was colder now, and the neighborhood looked bare with most of the leaves off the trees. Acorns popped under our bicycle wheels.

"You're doing it right now." Roger rode beside me. I kept my eyes straight ahead.

"You're going back there," he said, "because you think you're better than everybody else."

I rammed my bike into his, knocking us both onto the pavement, the bikes clattering around us. I stared up at the gray sky, then tried to get up, but my pants were tangled in my bike chain. I looked over to see Roger lying on the pavement too, leaning back on his elbows. His front wheel spun in the air. He was shaking his head, but he seemed to be shaking it at himself.

Roger pushed his bike off of himself and stood up, peeling leaves from his coat. I tried to untangle my pants from the chain. I pulled too hard and ripped the cuff. Roger stood over his front wheel, holding it between his knees, and straightened the handlebars. He looked sad.

"I don't do things so I can tell on myself," I said, examining the hole in my pants. "And neither did George Washington."

Roger didn't speak as he straightened a bent spoke in his wheel. I picked up my bike and began trying to replace the chain.

"My father is divorcing my mother," he said, his voice cracking. He held my bike for me while I fiddled with the chain. "He was going over to tell her after we left. He's probably telling her this very minute."

I didn't know what to say.

"Your father says my name weird," I said, still angry, turning the pedal to slip the chain into place.

Roger handed me my bike. "He says a lot of things weird." I looked over my shoulder in the direction of Miss Hawkins's house, but there was no sign of her. We climbed onto our bikes and pedaled slowly up Pine Forest.

"I shouldn't have said that about your father," I said.

We rode up the street in awkward silence. Finally Roger

frowned and said, "I never knew anybody who felt so strongly about the presidents."

We turned onto Crescent Avenue, a hushed street of ivied mansions, imposing hedges, and manicured lawns. It was a street we had ridden on a thousand times on our way to other places. This particular afternoon, it seemed especially Crescent Avenue–ish. The long driveways glistened with Lincolns and Cadillacs, and if there were any bikes in the yards, they were shiny English bikes with skinny tires and hand brakes. We rarely saw anyone outside, except for the yardmen.

The children who lived on this street attended Christ Church, the private Episcopal school. I sensed that they knew when we were coming and rushed inside, so as not to be seen with children of lesser streets.

Roger and I rode aimlessly now. We circled and swerved, performed figure eights, taking our time since Roger was in no hurry to get home. He seemed more depressed as we rode along, and I wondered what, if anything, I might do or say to shake him out of it.

We wound up in Cleveland Park, where Roger and I had spent at least half of our time last summer. It was a hundred-acre swath of land divided by the city's approximation of a river, the Reedy. Most of the park was wooded, with grassy paths beside the river. Occasional weeping willows draped themselves over the water, like giant girls washing their hair. In the center of the park was a large, open, flat field, where the city had put up swings, monkey bars, tennis courts, and picnic tables. Since this was also the city's floodplain, everything was often caked with a sour-smelling river mud.

Beside the river was an indoor roller-skating rink and,

connected to it, an outdoor pool, which, when desegrega-
tion finally began to be enforced, the city remodeled into a
seal pond rather than have Negro children swim with
white children.

On the other side of the parking lot, up on a hill safe
from floodwaters, was the Greenville zoo, a small collection of cages containing bored-looking rabbits, a grassless
town of prairie dogs, a mangy bobcat, and two ill-
tempered chimpanzees. Peacocks wandered between the
cages as if they were the keepers. My mother never went
with us to the zoo, saying that if anyone needed caging, it
was humans.

As we rode along the path that followed the river, we
passed a meadow with a jet plane mounted in the middle.
It was a silver spy plane, an F-86 Sabre fighter—a memor-
ial to a pilot from Greenville who had been shot down last
year during the Cuban Missile Crisis. He had been the
only American casualty. The plane was mounted ten feet
off the ground and tilted so that when you came around
the bend, it appeared to be flying right at you. Roger and I
had spent many afternoons reenacting the last moments of
the pilot's life as his plane spiraled toward its fiery doom.
But Roger didn't seem interested in the plane today. We
rode on past.

I decided that the only way to get his mind off his father
was to tell him something crucial, something I had never
told anyone. We walked our bikes onto an arched stone
bridge and looked down into the river. The Reedy River
was sluggish and polluted. Oil rainbows bloomed on its
shiny surface. A dark chemical smell wafted up to us. Old
tires, sludge-filled bottles, and smashed cans littered the
banks. Now and then there was a report of a carp or cat-

fish that had been caught, but for the most part it was a dead river. Still, a moving body of water was enough for us.

"If I told you a secret, would you promise not to tell?" I threw a piece of bark off the bridge and watched it drift slowly underneath.

"I know all your secrets." Roger gazed into the murky water.

"Mitchell didn't stop for that dog," I heard myself say. "He fell."

Roger kept staring into the water.

"Did you hear what I said?" I asked. "He didn't die like I said he did." I leaned toward him. "He tripped." The only sound was the rippling current below. "I'm not sure if I tripped him or not," I said, now caught up in my revelation. "I do know he fell and that he called out to me. I started to go back, but then I saw the dog coming, and I ran."

Roger looked at me for the first time. "You're not making this up?"

"We were running away from the dog, and Mitchell tripped somehow," I said. "I started back, but then I saw the dog coming fast." I zipped my jacket, starting to feel the cold again. "But what if I had stayed? What if we had fought the dog off together?"

"Whoa," Roger said quietly.

"When Aunt Louise and Uncle Clem asked what happened, I told them this other story. Mitchell would have tried to save me." A peacock's mournful cry echoed down from the zoo. "If I hadn't run," I said.

Roger didn't say anything else, but I could see by the way he kept looking at me that not only had I gotten his attention, but he wasn't quite sure he knew me anymore.

I would never be certain exactly what happened, but in the version I told Roger on the bridge, the version I felt I must believe, I presented the worst of me, in case it was the truth.

We climbed onto our bikes and headed home. We were both quiet now. My revelation might have distracted Roger momentarily, but he seemed to have gone back to his brooding. Streetlights buzzed on overhead as we rode the last couple of blocks toward home. I couldn't stop talking about my secret, now that I knew it.

"I am not sure whether I tripped Mitchell," I said again. "I didn't mean to, but I'm not sure if his foot caught mine. I just don't know. Does that make me crazy?"

"Crazy people don't understand they're crazy," said Roger flatly. "My father says some people claim to be crazy so they won't be blamed."

This made me feel even worse, raising the possibility that I was shirking responsibility. Of course, my attempts to implicate myself in my brother's death reinforced my belief that what had happened to Mitchell was something I had done, something I had had a choice about, something I had controlled. As a child, I did not dare entertain the truly frightening thought that life was capricious and utterly out of my hands.

Roger and I didn't speak, our bike shadows rolling silently beside us on the pavement. Then, without a word, he began pedaling faster and faster until he had left me behind. I didn't catch up. I didn't want to. I did turn onto Afton Avenue in time to see him walk his bike up his gravel driveway. He didn't call out good night or even glance back in my direction.

· · ·

MISS HAWKINS SAT AT HER DESK, correcting our homework, while we read about Central America. The smell of
salmon croquettes meant the hair-netted women in the
cafeteria were preparing lunch.

Without looking up from her book, Norma slid a folded
piece of paper across my desk. I unfolded it, and written
in her even, cursive handwriting was the sentence "I am
your half sister." I folded the paper, then opened it and
read it again. I looked at Norma. She leaned over in her
desk and whispered in my ear. "Mama told me. We have
the same father."

I looked down at the note again, read it again, then
looked at Norma again.

"Norma, do you and Jeru have something you would
like to share?" Miss Hawkins asked.

I slipped the piece of paper into my desk.

"No, ma'am." Norma picked up her book.

Miss Hawkins went back to grading papers, and I kept
thinking about the note.

At recess, I followed the other boys onto the playground. I took my usual position in the netherworld of the
outer outfield, where even the biggest boys couldn't hit
the ball. Norma walked by and motioned for me to follow
her. I hesitated.

"Come on." She waved me over to the old sycamore by
the fence.

I followed. She sat down on a big rock and patted for me
to sit down next to her, but I shook my head. "What does
that note mean?" I asked.

"What it says." Norma tore off a piece of the sycamore's
bark.

"Nobody ever said anything about me having a sister," I said.

"I'm a secret." Norma leaned against the tree trunk. The word sounded in my head like a bell. I remembered the letter I had flushed down the toilet and how my father had asked me to keep his secret.

"Mama says you have a brother," Norma said.

"His name is Henry," I said, watching across the field where Ricky McIntire had come up to bat.

"Mama says your father used to work for an advertising agency but she's not sure what he does now."

"He's writing a book," I said, still not looking at her.

"Your mother writes too. Mama showed me her name on articles in the paper."

"She's going to have a baby," I said, my tone becoming more irritated, as if I were reminding her I knew more about my family than she did.

She studied me a minute. "We didn't move here to follow y'all," she said. "We moved here for Mama's work." She picked at a scab on her hand. "Telling you was my idea."

"Somebody would have told me if I had a sister," I said.

"I'm telling you." She stood, still scratching the back of her hand. "I am your sister." She ran to join the girls playing kickball on the grass beside the jungle gym. She kept looking back at me. The boys called to me that it was my turn to bat, but I sat on the rock where Norma had been and thought about how she never got anything wrong.

· · ·

BEWILDERED, I STOPPED SPEAKING TO NORMA for a week. I didn't understand how the skinny little tough girl who had been sitting next to me since last year could possibly be related to me. At school, I walked around in a daze. At night, I tried to read, but my mind kept veering to Norma. I couldn't shake the image of her walking up to our house, suitcase in hand. I imagined her pausing at the front door, as if trying to make up her mind, then ringing the doorbell, and, as she did, the house blowing apart, a miniature mushroom cloud in its place.

A few days later, Miss Hawkins was talking in the hallway to Mrs. Roberts, the librarian, when Miss Hawkins asked me to step into the hall. Roger and I exchanged glances. We had been waiting for this. Most likely Mrs. Roberts had finally told Miss Hawkins she had spotted us pedaling away from her house. We had decided, too, that Mrs. Roberts would probably recognize me and not Roger from a distance, because I was rounder, more distinct in shape.

When I walked into the hall, Mrs. Roberts had left, and Miss Hawkins was alone. "I'm sorry," I blurted.

Miss Hawkins told the class to continue reading, then she guided me down the hall, the clip of her shoes echoing through the building. I supposed we were headed to Mr. Keener's office, but we turned away from his office and walked up the stairs to the second-floor library, which was eerily empty. Miss Hawkins sat down at Mrs. Roberts's desk.

By this time, I was so terrified, tears welled in my eyes. "Miss Hawkins, I am very sorry," I said.

She slid a book across the desk to me. It was *John F. Kennedy and PT-109.* On top of the book lay the checkout card on which we printed our names. "Yours is the last name on the card."

I picked up the card. In fact, mine was the only name on the card. I had checked it out half a dozen times, reading and rereading the chapters entitled "Disaster at Sea" and "Shipwrecked on an Island," which described how Kennedy, after having his PT boat run over by a Japanese destroyer, endured great pain and suffering, walking barefoot on foot-slicing coral and swimming miles through shark-infested waters, all for the sake of saving his crew.

Underneath my name on the card, written in what appeared to be my handwriting, was the sentence "I don't want anything to do with poor white trash." It filled up the rest of the card.

I held the card, staring at it while trying to get my bearings. This was not about Miss Hawkins's broken picture—something I had done. It was about writing on the library card—something I had not done. My dread shifted into uncertainty. I stared at the card, wondering who would have written it? Ricky McIntire. He liked practical jokes, but this was too subtle and the spelling too correct.

"I must say, when Mrs. Roberts brought this to my attention I couldn't believe that you would write such a hateful thing." Miss Hawkins folded her hands on the desk. "It does resemble your handwriting." She emphasized the word "resemble" as if she was not certain I had written it.

I handed the card back. "I didn't write that."

"Why did you tell me you were sorry? You seemed to know what I was talking about."

I looked at my feet. I considered telling her about our trespassing in her house and my breaking her picture, but that would have incriminated Roger, who had enough on his mind. Also, if I turned us in, I would never hear the end of it from Roger.

I looked up at Miss Hawkins and, staring her right in the eye, spoke in the steadiest voice I could muster, "I did not write that."

Miss Hawkins and I stared at each other for what felt like an hour. Outside, a car horn honked. The march of footsteps passed by the library door—Mrs. Davis's sixth grade on its way to lunch. My heart had moved up into my head and was pounding behind my eyeballs, but I refused to look away, knowing that if I did, all was lost.

She was the one who looked away. She laid her hands flat on the desk and stared at them, then picked up the card. "I believe you," she said. "It isn't in you to be so malicious." She sounded as if she had taken the note on the library card personally, which I would have understood had I been able to think past my guilt about her broken picture and remember who it had been a picture of and where it had been taken.

She rose from the desk, wandered over to the window, and looked out; it was a gray, rainy day and all the leaves had fallen, making for a slick, stark world. The radiators knocked. Miss Hawkins had seemed troubled lately. She looked very tired, and I began to grow uncomfortable, standing there.

"I will find out who wrote it," she said, still looking out the window. "I can see into the hearts of all my students." She walked over to the biography section and brushed her fingers along the titles. Then she squinted at me as if she had X-ray vision. "For instance, you have your dead brother."

"Ma'am?"

"That is why you read these." She pulled a biography from the shelf. "Every time you read about a person, you raise him from the dead, bring him back to life within the covers of the book. You read to resurrect."

"Vessie?" Mrs. Roberts was standing in the doorway, a puzzled expression on her face. I didn't know how long she had been there.

Miss Hawkins walked back to the desk and picked up the library card. "Jeru did not write this."

Mrs. Roberts apologized for the mix-up, then Miss Hawkins sent me back to the room, while she stayed behind and talked to Mrs. Roberts. I remember feeling real exhilaration as I walked back. I had faced Miss Hawkins, had resisted telling on myself, and by so doing had protected both Roger and me. After I finished recounting to Roger what had happened, he asked, "Who did write on the library card?"

Norma, who had been sitting quietly reading, glanced up from her book, smiled too innocently, then went back to her reading. Roger gave me an uncomprehending shrug.

"You?" I asked her, but she didn't look up. "You almost got me in a lot of trouble."

She snapped her book shut. "It's true, isn't it?" She curled her lip at me, giving me the same fierce look she gave Miss Hawkins whenever she corrected her grammar. "You don't want anything to do with white trash."

"I don't think you're white trash," I said, surprised by Norma's vehemence.

"Humph." Norma picked up her book again and, twirling her hair around her finger, pretended to read.

"I really don't think you're white trash," I said, feeling the other children turn in their seats.

Roger nudged me in the ribs, and the room hushed as we heard Miss Hawkins's brisk footsteps marching up the hall toward us.

CHAPTER FIVE

Taking Della Home

AT FIRST, THE NEWS of the president being shot diverted my attention from Norma's claim of kinship. I remember Mr. Keener's announcement to the class—how some of us gasped, how others cried "No!" Millicent Dillingham, a strange girl who somehow still believed in Santa Claus, who wasn't allowed to watch TV, and whose parents had voted for Nixon, said, "Good," then burst into tears.

As we filed down the school steps, out onto the front walk, the older children looked shocked, but the younger children were excited, jostling one another, ecstatic to be freed early.

At the bottom of the steps, Norma stopped me. "I'm sorry, Jeru," she said, her schoolbooks tucked under her arm. "I know how much you like the president." It was the first time she had spoken to me since the library-book incident. I didn't say anything as she turned up the sidewalk in the direction of Augusta Road.

Roger and I walked home together, neither of us talking for a few blocks, too stunned by the news.

"I hope he wasn't shot in a vital organ," Roger said finally.

"A vital organ?" I asked.

"Something you can't live without, like your heart or your liver."

"Maybe he was hit in the hand," I said. "Or the arm. Maybe the bullet grazed him."

"Maybe," Roger said, as we came to a patrol boy who walked us across an intersection. We both knew that we wouldn't be getting out of school an hour early for a flesh wound.

The streets were a blur on the way home. I didn't see the juniper bush until I had walked right into it, scratching my face on its branches.

I was so upset that I resorted to Christian Science, or my version of it. If anybody was the Divine Reflection of God, it most certainly had to be the president. Therefore, a material object, like a bullet from a gun, could not have any power over him.

"Maybe a Russian spy shot him," I said sometime later.

"Maybe it's the start of an atomic war." Roger squinted into the sky, pulling his dog tag from underneath his shirt. I pulled mine out too, pressing the cold metal in my palm. We had all been issued tags with our names and addresses stamped on them. It was explained they were in case we were ever lost. I suspected a darker reason.

At home, I headed straight to my room, tossed my knapsack onto my bed, hung my coat in my closet, and paused in front of the framed photograph of Kennedy. He was still smiling at his desk. I found Henry in his room, holding a dead monarch butterfly in his palm. He had been sent home early as well.

"Can you believe it?" I sat on the edge of his bed.

"What?" Henry held the butterfly as if it was flying.

"The president." I stared at a bleached jawbone of a possum that Henry had found in McKissick's Creek. On the same shelf was a bird skull, a ribbed turtle shell, and a very large cow bone he'd found in some field. From the time he was a toddler, Henry had a fascination with dead things—not because he was morbid, but because of the lives their remains suggested.

Henry carefully set the butterfly on a shelf with various jars of dead insects.

"Do you know where he was shot?" I opened and closed a blue crab's claw.

Henry picked up a bleached turtle shell. "Box turtles are good at getting away. They can even dig under fences."

I found Della in the den. She was pressing one of my father's white shirts and watching television. Smoke curled from a cigarette in an ashtray she kept at the end of the ironing board. This was Della's station every afternoon. In the mornings, she cleaned the house, then washed our clothes and hung them on the line out back. In the afternoons, she brought in the laundry and ironed in front of the television, watching her stories. I only had to see an episode every year or so to keep up with the plots. But even if I was in some other part of the house or on my way outside, I caught bits of the stilted dialogue or a swell of melodramatic music.

There were tears in her eyes.

"So you heard?" I asked.

She put her finger to her lips, and I followed her gaze to the television, where a woman I recognized as a character on *Edge of Night* had come out of a hospital room, dabbing her eyes with a handkerchief.

"Do you know the president has been shot?" I asked, as a ketchup commercial came on.

"They's been interrupting my program every now and then." Della took a puff of her cigarette. "They say he got shot in the head."

Roger and I hadn't even thought about the possibility of a head wound. "Does Daddy know?" I nodded to the typing coming up from the basement.

"I told him when they first announce it. He say keep him posted." Della picked up her iron again, as *Edge of Night* came back on the television.

I was exasperated with the casual way my family had taken the news. I went to the kitchen pantry to the shelf devoted to Marshmallow Pinwheels, Devilcake Squares, Fig Newtons, and Cameos. I stood at the kitchen counter eating cookies and drinking milk as if it was slugs of gin.

An announcer's voice had come on the television saying that they were interrupting the regularly scheduled program for a special news bulletin. Then there was Walter Cronkite, looking as sober as Mr. Keener.

"Oh my Lord," Della said, setting down the hissing iron. Henry came out of his room, and the two of us sat on the couch. Della ran to the top of the basement steps and called down. "Mr. Lamb!" I heard my father run up the stairs. "They say he dead." My father came in, holding a cigarette.

"What the world coming to, Mr. Lamb?" Della wiped her eyes with a handkerchief she'd started to iron.

"I wish I knew." My father pulled a chair out from the breakfast table and sat.

I got up.

"Where you going, Jeru?" Della asked.

I walked through the kitchen and out the side door. At first I was walking, then walking faster, then trotting, then running as hard as my legs would carry me up the middle of Afton Avenue. No one was around. Everyone was inside listening to the details, as if going over the way it had happened might bring him back or, at the very least, make sense out of something that I knew firsthand made less sense the more you thought about it. I ran until I had to stop at the top of the street, sit down on the curb, and catch my breath. And then for reasons I am still not sure of, I began to pound my thigh so hard that I later had bruises.

A strong hand squeezed my shoulder, and I looked up into my father's tired eyes. "I wish she wasn't having this baby," I said.

In the distance there was a siren, and the neighborhood dogs howled. The wind picked up, scuttling the leaves along the gutter. My father sat beside me on the curb—and instead of trying to say something to make me feel better, something I would not have believed—he just sat beside me and waited.

IF IT HADN'T BEEN FOR THE ASSASSINATION, my father would not have forgotten to remove the blue letter from the mail that afternoon; my mother would not have been so distracted that night when she came home that she accidentally opened and read something addressed to him.

The evening of the assassination, we had been on our way back from taking Della home. My father, driving his 1959 Lincoln, sat up front alone after Della got out. Henry and I spread out across the endless backseat. It was only a fifteen-minute drive from our house to West Greenville, where Della lived, but it was almost an hour bus ride, because the bus went downtown first and then Della had to wait for a transfer. On Fridays when Della did her shopping, she took the bus downtown after work, but otherwise my father or my mother gave her a ride home.

After we dropped off Della, my father wound his way through the maze of narrow, unmarked alleys and streets that made up West Greenville. Even with the night chill, Negroes stood out on their porches talking or yelling over to neighbors at the next house, as they did almost every night. My father had to drive slowly because of the children. Negro children owned their streets. I always looked forward to our nightly rattling across the railroad tracks into this darker, exotic country of raked dirt yards and tiny, inviting houses on cinder blocks.

My mother had supper on the table by the time we returned. She seemed unusually quiet this night, as she set our plates in front of us, but we were all quiet—even Henry seemed more thoughtful. We ate with the television on, watching Huntley and Brinkley, two men I admired almost as much as I admired Lewis and Clark. They looked haggard, and the whole broadcast was devoted to the assassination. The Dallas police had found a suspect in a movie theater.

In the middle of the meal, my mother threw down her napkin, shoved her chair back, and trotted off to their bedroom, closing the door behind her. We thought she was upset about the assassination. She had done the same thing many times after Mitchell died. My father went to see her but found the bedroom door locked, and when he tried talking to her through the door, she slid the opened blue letter underneath the door.

"Aw, Muriel," my father said, picking up the letter. He jiggled the doorknob. He stood there, his ear pressed against the door. After a while, he came back in the den where Henry and I were finishing our supper. "Can you boys take care of the dishes?" He walked back to the bedroom and knocked again. When there was no reply, he descended the stairs to his office.

I washed, and Henry dried as best he could. We went to our rooms, he to rearrange his shell collection and I to read a book about Eli Whitney, who was in the middle of inventing the cotton gin. The clatter of my father's typing was the only sound in the house.

When my father didn't come back up and my mother didn't leave her room, I went into Henry's room to tell him to get into his pajamas, but he was lying on his bed, already wearing them.

"Have you brushed your teeth?" I asked.

He nodded, handing me a conch shell we had bought at a shop in Myrtle Beach. Henry held a smaller conch shell against his ear. "Is Mama mad at Daddy?" he asked.

"I think so," I said, putting the shell to my ear and listening to the distant roar of the ocean. I remembered sitting on the balcony of the Wee Blue Inn with Mitchell at night, watching the moon shine a yellow path across the dark water.

"Why is she mad?" asked Henry.

"I don't know." I handed the shell back to him, then I turned out the light, leaving on a circular greenish nightlight next to his bed. "When we go into the army," he asked, "will we have to spend the night?"

"Probably." I picked up his stuffed elephant from the foot of the bed and handed it to him.

He pulled the covers up to his chin and stared at the ceiling.

Later that night, I was awakened by my parents' bedroom door opening. I heard my mother tiptoe into Henry's room, check on him, and then tiptoe into mine. I pretended to be asleep as she tugged the covers up around me. She walked slowly down the basement stairs. It wasn't long before I heard my parents' voices. I slipped out of bed and stood by the basement door. But I couldn't hear them clearly, so I tiptoed down the basement stairs.

My mother was standing at the door to my father's office, in one of his flannel shirts and her slip, which bulged with the baby to come, her hair disheveled. All I could see of my father was a wisp of smoke coming out of his office.

"I didn't mean to open it," she said, pushing her hair back. "One minute I was opening bills and then the next minute I was reading about my husband's daughter, my husband's wife. . . . How could you, Warren?"

"It was before you, before our family. I thought I loved her . . ."

"I mean how could you leave them? How could you walk out on her?"

There was a long pause. "That was when I met you, when I knew I was in love with you."

"That is so selfish," she said. "How could you fall in love with anyone else when there was this woman having your baby?"

I tiptoed down another step.

"Would you rather our family hadn't happened?" he asked.

"I'd rather you had been honest from the beginning." She rolled her head against the door, eyeing him. She pulled the flannel shirt around her.

"I don't blame you for wanting to find your daughter," she said, her voice softening. But then it hardened again: "I blame you for keeping secrets." She frowned at the charcoal sketches pinned up all over his office. "Who are these women anyway?"

I stood there, knowing more than ever that Norma had told the truth about who she was.

My mother watched my father, and just when I was sure she was about to be really angry, she yawned. "The newspaper was busy today. It is inconceivable that Kennedy is dead."

"It upset Jeru . . ." I could tell by my father's voice that he was happy to talk about something else, and suddenly I wanted out of there, not wanting to hear about me.

"He worshiped Kennedy. Sometimes I worry about Jeru. He takes everything to heart." She yawned a long yawn. "I have to get some sleep. Tomorrow will probably be even busier. Are you coming to bed?"

"I'll be up in a little while." My father didn't resume typing at first as she walked slowly up the stairs. I tiptoed quickly back upstairs and into my room. I heard her go into the bathroom and brush her teeth.

I climbed into bed, surprised that my parents hadn't argued more, that my mother hadn't packed her suitcase and called a cab in the middle of the night as I had seen one irate wife do on *As the World Turns.* My mother hadn't even made my father sleep on the couch, like Roger's father had done before he moved out. I lay there, trying to understand how, when terrible things happened and the end of the world was imminent, adults could brush their teeth and go to bed.

I stared at the photograph of Kennedy over my bed and pondered how he had survived the sinking of his PT boat, swimming miles in shark-infested waters, and hiding out for days on an island in enemy territory only to be shot in broad daylight riding along a street in Texas. Where was the president tonight? Was he in a mortuary? Cold and alone with a sheet pulled over him? Now the entire country was going through what my family had been going through ever since Mitchell died. Now the entire nation knew how we felt. Now we weren't so conspicuous.

CHAPTER SIX

Confusion to the Enemy

EVERY YEAR, BEGINNING A COUPLE of weeks before Thanksgiving, my mother kept longer hours at the newspaper to cover the school concerts, food drives, toy drives, Christmas caroling, and other holiday events. This year was no exception. Most nights she didn't return home until eight or eight-thirty. Although my father worried about her overworking in her condition, it gave him a chance to prove himself by cooking for us and putting us to bed.

Also, it provided a break from the disquiet that had settled over the house. As far as I knew, my mother hadn't mentioned the letter again. Perhaps her reticence was her way of making him feel guilty, or maybe she had decided that she had said enough. I could never be sure about the motives of adults; everything they did or didn't do seemed unnecessarily complicated.

My mother would come home to a chicken pot pie or fish sticks warming in the oven and my father typing in the basement. She would check on Henry, then me. Smelling of newsroom cigarette smoke, she would sit on my bed and recount her day, talk she usually reserved for my father. She discussed stories she had written, people she had interviewed, meetings she had attended. Best of all, she would tell me what mischief Dennis the Menace would be up to in tomorrow's comics.

Sometimes when she finished telling me about the paper, I asked her questions that I had been mulling over.

"Is everybody really the reflection of God?"

"Yes."

"So if President Kennedy was the reflection of God, why did he die?"

"Death is an illusion."

"Like a dream?"

"Sort of."

"We dreamed he was shot?"

"In a way."

"All of us? How could a whole country, a whole world, have the same dream?"

"Mortal Mind."

I would sit up on my pillow. "Mortal Mind is everywhere."

She sighed to herself. "All over the front page."

"But if we dreamed the president is dead, where is he really? Where did he really go? Where did Mitchell really go?"

Sometimes she wouldn't answer. She would sit silently for a long time. "The baby is kicking." She would take my hand and place it on her belly, and I would feel something graze my hand, like a fish, quick and gone. For her, this signal from within was a real comfort, but I had grown distrustful of what I could not see.

She would kiss my forehead and say good night. Sometimes she would open the door to the basement and stand there, listening to my father type. My father never came up while I was awake. He had nearly finished his book, and sometimes I woke at two or three in the morning and heard the faint clatter coming up through the floor. It was a hopeful sound.

MISS HAWKINS'S MENTAL DETERIORATION had been gradual, a subtle wearing away. However, during the latter part of November, her air of distraction became obvious enough for even us fifth graders. The assassination had definitely thrown her. She began to forget from day to day what she had assigned as homework. When she performed long division on the board, she would stop mid-problem and stare at her figures as if they were hieroglyphics. During our geography lesson, she would pull down the map and point to countries whose names escaped her.

We anticipated school with morbid curiosity, wondering what Miss Hawkins was going to forget next. Magically, the tables had been turned, and now she was the one being tested. It never occurred to me how terrifying this must have been for Miss Hawkins, a woman who had spent her life knowing all the answers and who now had to resort to the back of the book.

The day before Thanksgiving, Miss Hawkins was at the board, writing a list of words for us to copy and memorize over the holidays. Roger nudged me. "She has misspelled about half the words," he whispered.

"Shouldn't we tell her?" I asked.

Roger stared at me. "You're crazier than any loony on Bull Street."

My father appeared in the classroom doorway, dressed in a coat and tie. An alarm went off in my head. Something had happened to my mother or Henry or Aunt Louise or Uncle Clem. He held up my forgotten lunch box.

"Jeru." Miss Hawkins had noticed my father in the doorway. She motioned me up front. She straightened the papers on her desk. "We were about to have a little spelling lesson, Mr. Lamb."

"Is that him?" Norma leaned over, whispering in my ear. Her eyes were wide, and she seemed ready to jump out of her desk.

"Don't let me interrupt." My father glanced at the board, but I couldn't tell if he noticed the misspellings.

"Miss Hawkins." Norma waved her hand frantically, looking in my father's direction. "Some of those words are misspelled."

Miss Hawkins turned around, saw who had spoken, looked back at the board, and gave an audible sigh.

"You left the *h* off 'schedule.' " Norma sounded almost hysterical. "The *g* off 'enough.' 'Separate' has two *a*'s . . ." She talked to Miss Hawkins but stared the whole time at my father.

"Why don't you come up and correct them, Norma?" Miss Hawkins turned to my father. "We all make mistakes, don't we, Mr. Lamb?" She was trying to make light of her misspellings, but we could tell she was shaken.

My father handed me my lunch box. "Does Miss Hawkins usually misspell words?" he whispered, watching Norma walk up to the board.

I shook my head.

He studied Miss Hawkins a minute, then bent down and whispered into my ear, "Confusion to the enemy." He patted my shoulder and started to leave, but I followed him into the hall.

"She's acting real funny, Daddy," I said, keeping my voice low.

He looked at me a moment, no longer smiling. He watched Miss Hawkins, who was standing beside Norma at the board and smiling in a strange way. He nodded at me. I let go of his hand and watched him walk down the hall with that crisp, pigeon-toed bounce of his. I almost called to him but instead ran back to my desk. Miss Hawkins folded her arms, still watching Norma.

"She is going to kill her." Roger buried his head on his desk. "Can't look."

Norma erased Miss Hawkins's mistakes and began to rewrite the words, looking crestfallen that my father had left. I found myself reaching into my pocket, feeling the shape of my pocketknife.

"Norma is an intelligent girl, isn't she, class?"

"Tell me when it's over," Roger whispered, his head still in his arms. But Miss Hawkins didn't yank Norma's arm or even flick her ear. Instead, she patted her shoulder. "Norma was the only one who had the courage to correct me."

Roger and I looked at each other in disbelief, and for a moment it seemed that whatever danger there might have been had miraculously passed. Norma finished correcting the words on the board and went back to her desk. Miss Hawkins stared at the words for a long time as if they were faces she was trying to place, then she sat at her desk. She picked up an empty blue flower vase, turning it over in her hands. The longer she stared at the vase, the more uneasy we became.

She held up the vase for us to see. "A student in my

first class gave me this," she said in a quiet voice. "I was teaching before most of your parents were born." She removed her glasses and rubbed her eyes, then put the glasses back on.

She walked to the board, picked up an eraser, and mechanically wiped away the corrected words. She faced the board for such a long time that we began to whisper among ourselves.

She turned around, her face as blank as the board behind her. "I know you," she said to us quietly as she began to pace the aisles. "I know you all." She placed her hand on Ricky McIntire's head. "I know your hopes. I know your dreams." Her tone was too intimate, reminding me of the way she had spoken to me in the library. "I know what it is that each of you longs for more than anything in the world," her voice trembled. In parting some curtain in herself, she was revealing too much.

She pressed her clenched fist against her chest and said, "I know the forces of your heart."

Feeling something was amiss, my father had fetched Mr. Keener, and the two of them had come up to the doorway and were watching.

Miss Hawkins walked over to Norma at her desk and gently took her hand, turned it over, and traced the lines in her palm like a fortune-teller. "I know you long for your dead father. I see the loss in your eyes, in the way you carry yourself, in your voice."

Norma rose from her desk, a frightened expression on her face. She backed away from Miss Hawkins, but slipped, fell, and hit her head hard on Billy Bukowski's desk. She lay in the aisle, blinking and rubbing her head. I ran up to Norma, bending down beside her.

"Everything looks all fuzzy." Norma leaned against me, but before I knew what was happening my father was beside us, lifting Norma into his arms.

"Could I have a word with you, Miss Hawkins?" Mr. Keener took our teacher firmly by the elbow, led her out into the hall, and never brought her back.

DR. NORTON SHINED HIS PENLIGHT into Norma's eyes. He was a kind man with gentle hands, an easy manner, and a bald, freckled head.

Norma sat on the examining table, nervously swinging her feet. "My head has gone for a walk," she said.

My father and I stood at the door of the examining room.

"Honey, the brain is a bowlful of Jell-O," the doctor said, "and yours has been shaken up."

"A bowlful of Jell-O?" Norma touched her head gingerly.

My father patted his shirt for his cigarettes, took out the pack, then, remembering he was in the doctor's office, put the pack back. Dr. Norton's office was in an old house close to downtown. My father had volunteered to drive Norma over, after the school nurse said Norma might have a concussion. Norma had told us her mother was at the Belk store in Spartanburg today and wouldn't be home until the late afternoon. The whole ride over, I kept expecting Norma, who sat in the backseat holding an ice pack to her forehead, to reveal to my father who she was.

Dr. Norton bounced his little rubber hammer on Norma's knee. "Close your eyes and touch your finger to your nose," he said.

She closed her eyes and touched her right finger to her nose, then her left.

Dr. Norton slipped his stethoscope under Norma's

blouse and onto her bare chest. I found myself staring. Her blouse was untucked, not unbuttoned, but I could see the hint of breast underneath.

I backed out of the examining room. My father went to try calling Norma's mother, in case she had gotten home early, and I sat in the waiting room. Dr. Norton's waiting room was a large space with straight-backed chairs and a table with two-year-old magazines in the middle. As usual, it was crowded with whites and a few Negroes. Dr. Norton was one of a handful of white doctors who treated Negroes. He also didn't charge patients who couldn't afford to pay.

Because he had so many patients and because he was thorough, it wasn't unusual to have to wait an hour or two. My mother usually brought us. Although she no longer believed in medicine for herself, she did not have enough confidence in her newfound belief to risk her children, so, much to our disappointment, she insisted we have our checkups and our shots.

As I sat in the waiting room, leafing through a tattered copy of *Look,* I felt a deep sadness. I was sitting in a roomful of sick people—some coughed, some held their heads or rubbed their eyes, and one little girl couldn't stop crying. Worse than the people was the smell of alcohol, which masked all the darker smells. The same smell had been in my mother's clothes after she had returned from the hospital, having seen Mitchell.

I couldn't sit anymore. I went over to the full Indian headdress that stood in a dusty glass case in the corner. The case was covered with children's handprints. Mitchell and I used to press against the case, imagining the fierce chief who once wore the headdress. I pressed my fingers on a clear set of prints slightly smaller than my own and wondered if they were Mitchell's.

THE DAY MY BROTHER IS KILLED, Aunt Louise calls home after she calls an ambulance. My father is the only one there, having just gotten back from a tennis match in Cleveland Park. My mother has taken Henry to a movie, but no one knows which theater. My father beats the ambulance to Clem and Louise's.

Louise meets him at the door and shows him into the den, where Clem has lain Mitchell on the cot. They had told me to wait in the kitchen, but I watch by cracking the swinging door. No one speaks. Clem stands beside Mitchell with his hat in his hand. His breathing is labored, having beaten off the dog and carried Mitchell up through the garden and into the house. The television is on a base-ball game.

I can't see my father's face as he bends over the body. He is in his tennis shorts and shoes. Clem puts his hand on my father's shoulder. My father holds Mitchell's wrist, feeling for a pulse, then he kneels and lays his head against Mitchell's chest, listening. He pushes Mitchell's hair off his forehead. In all the chaos of the dog and the Negro boys and the shooting, I had not really seen Mitchell's face. I see it now.

My father shakes his head at Mitchell and whispers. "Oh, honey, what are we going to tell your mother?" As if Mitchell has gotten his Sunday clothes muddy before church.

"Were you able to reach Muriel?" Louise asks.

"No." He strokes Mitchell's forehead. "There's no hurry now. Is there, my boy?" He leans over and pulls Mitchell against him, bloodying his tennis whites.

I run out from behind the kitchen door and throw myself around my father's neck. He hugs me and Mitchell at the same time. I bury my face in my father's shirt, smelling sweat and cigarette smoke.

When we hear the ambulance, my father scoops Mitchell into his arms, and my brother's head lolls back, showing a big cut across his throat. His hand falls loose, grazing my cheek. Louise, Clem, and I follow my father outside. The siren brings neighbors into their yards. The attendants hurry over to my father. One of them pushes Mitchell's eyes open, takes one look, and shakes his head. They strap Mitchell onto a stretcher and wheel him into the ambulance. My father asks if he can ride with them. Louise, Clem, and I stand on the curb as they close the doors on my father and my brother.

"I'll call the movie theaters," Louise yells to him. "I'll find her."

My father raises his hand, but he is looking down at Mitchell. We watch the ambulance circle the campus, disappearing and reappearing through the trees, leaving much more slowly than it arrived. Its red light flashes, but now there is no siren.

The phone rings inside. "Jeru, run answer that," Aunt Louise says. "If it's your mother, I'll talk to her." I run into the house and pick up the receiver.

"Jeru?" My mother's voice. "Has something happened? I came home and found the front door wide open."

"Mitchell's hurt."

"Is he all right?"

"The dog, Mama." My face crumbles, my voice cracks. "I didn't think that chain would ever break . . ."

"Where is Aunt Louise?"

Louise takes the receiver. Clem leads me to the kitchen, where he sits me down at the kitchen table. He hands me his bandanna. I dab my eyes and blow my nose while he washes the brown dried blood from his hands at the kitchen sink. He limps over to the refrigerator, takes out a carton of buttermilk, and fills a jelly glass. He opens his pocketknife and cuts a wedge of the corn bread Aunt Louise had made the night before. He sets the corn bread and the milk in front of me and sits at the table, too. His face is pale, and his hand shakes as he lights a cigarette.

"Drink up, son." He nods at the glass of buttermilk. "You're going to need your strength. Today is going to be a long day."

I am not the least bit hungry, but somehow I drink the entire glass of buttermilk and eat every crumb of corn bread.

Louise walks into the kitchen and doesn't even look at us but braces herself at the sink, staring out the window.

"What'd you say to her?" Clem asks.

Louise stares out the window. Wisps of her long gray hair have escaped her hair clip, and her glasses rest crookedly on her nose. "She's meeting them at the emergency room." She turns to Clem. "The boy was right here in this kitchen not an hour ago, asking me to have a glass of iced tea with him. I told him I was sewing buttons and for him to run out and play." Aunt Louise's eyes redden.

There is a knock at the back door. Clem gets up, and I go with him. Mr. Blakely stands with his hat in one hand and Uncle Clem's .22 rifle that he had left in the garden in the other. The two boys who had tried to pull the dog off Mitchell stand at the foot of the steps, their heads bowed.

"I is awful, awful sorry what done happened here, Mr. Marshbanks." The old man hands Uncle Clem his rifle. "In seven years that old dog ain't hurt a fly. If'n they's anything we can do—"

"Anything you can do? Anything you can do?" Uncle Clem's face blushes to a beet red. "Listen here, Blakely! I been complaining about that dog ever since you first chained it up out there by that old oak. A dog like that is a menace. And every time I mentioned it, you said he was harmless. Now this happened."

Aunt Louise comes up behind her brother.

"This ain't something to be sorry about," says Uncle Clem. "It's a child. My nephew." He looks at the gun he holds and then at Mr. Blakely, but Aunt Louise slides it gently out of his hands as if she reads his mind. "Blakely," she says, "you better get on home."

"I'd like to get the dog," says the old man.

Aunt Louise nods.

The old man walks quickly down the steps and across the garden, his grandchildren trotting to keep up with him.

"Are you out of your mind?" Aunt Louise shakes the gun at Clem.

"I didn't do anything."

Aunt Louise opens the chamber in a way that shows she knows her way around guns. I have never even seen her hold a gun before. She unloads it, sets the safety, and props it against the sink.

"Blakely's got no business keeping a vicious dog," Uncle Clem says, sitting at the table.

"That dog wasn't vicious to Negroes," Louise says. "The boys were throwing rocks."

"Boys throw rocks, it ain't a capital offense. Whose side you on anyway?"

"The truth is, we're all at fault here. Mitchell was in our care. We have known about that dog for years." Louise walks out of the kitchen, down the hallway, and I hear the front door slam.

"Eh, Lawd," Clem says, sighing to himself.

I leave the table and walk down the back steps and along the garden path to the toolshed. I slide the stick out of the latch and open the doors. I take down my hoe and begin hoeing the lettuce, but when I look across the garden, I see the old man and the two boys dragging the big dog's body back down the Moores' field and across the creek. It takes all three of them, and even then the dog keeps slipping out of their hands, flopping into the high grass. The boys wipe their eyes. At some point I realize that they are crying for their dog.

I hoe for what feels like hours. I hoe until my arms ache and blisters form on my palms. Every now and then Clem or Louise comes out onto the back porch and calls to me. I don't answer. I continue scraping up weeds and dirt, not wanting to think or feel anything except the ground I churn up. I want to make myself useful. I hoe out the corn and the beans and am almost finished with the okra when my mother walks down to the garden.

"Let's go inside." She stands there, her eyes tearful and her makeup smeared.

"Did you see him?" I ask.

She nods, walking with me to the toolshed.

I try to keep my face from crumbling as I put away the hoe and close the doors to the toolshed. We start toward the house. Withered corn plants and shriveled pole beans border the path. My mother pulls me against her. "Oh, honey," she whispers. I am not sure if she is speaking to Mitchell or to me.

She shakes with convulsions. I hug her, my arms trembling from hoeing. I don't know how long we stand there—long enough for chill bumps to rise on my arms from the evening breeze, long enough for the dog to lunge at Mitchell a hundred more times, long enough for a fingernail moon to rise over the trees and slit the sky.

AFTER WE LEFT DR. NORTON'S OFFICE, Norma sat in the front seat with my father. She had nudged me aside when we were getting in. As we drove her home, I sat in the back and waited for her to lower the boom. Norma kept glancing at my father. Dr. Norton had put a small bandage on her forehead, saying she should be fine in a day or two. She shivered and turned up her coat collar. The rain had stopped, giving way to a gray chilly afternoon. Traffic was heavy.

As we were leaving the office, Dr. Norton took my father aside. I overheard him say he was concerned about my mother and her Christian Science. He told my father he needed to impress upon my mother that she should have a C-section and that a vaginal delivery was out of the question, would put mother and baby at risk.

I rode alone in the backseat, wondering why everything kept leading back to this. Was it God's way of making us pay attention to those dear to us, threatening us with their loss? Before Mitchell died, I had taken my family for granted. Now I could hardly think about my parents or Henry without also feeling the hollow weight of what it would be like to lose them. They had become fragile presences who meant too much.

"What is your book about?" Norma asked my father.

I sat up in my seat, dumbfounded. The question had never occurred to me. All the times I had stood in the doorway of his office listening to him type, I hadn't really cared what he was writing. His typing had seemed a worthy end in itself.

"Nothing, really." My father steered the car with one hand and glanced over at Norma beside him.

"I thought every book was about something." Norma frowned, her bandage wrinkling.

"I suppose that's true."

"Well, what happens in your book?"

My father shrugged. "Very little."

Norma looked out the window, as we turned down Augusta Road, passing Claussen's Bakery, where there was a big billboard of a smiling girl tearing a piece of white bread into two perfect halves. But Norma wasn't smiling. From what I could see of her face, she looked confused. "I will write a book someday," she said finally. She looked at my father. "All about me."

"I look forward to reading it," said my father, whose casual tone made Norma turn away and look out the window. "Maybe your mother is home by now," he said, pulling onto Mill's Avenue.

"She won't be home," she said, as if she better not be. Norma seemed nervous as we drove down the street, getting closer to her house. "You can let me out on this corner," she said, her hand on the door handle.

But naturally my father insisted on taking her to her door.

"She's not here," Norma sounded relieved as we pulled in front of a small mill house. I must admit I felt disappointed, hoping that this secret could have been dispensed with in one shocking meeting. Instead, we walked her to the door and waited while she picked up a key from under the doormat. She quickly opened the door and then, reassuring my father that she would be fine until her mother returned, disappeared inside.

When my father and I finally pulled onto Afton Avenue and I saw our lighted house set back in the trees, I thought how a few minutes earlier I had stood on the porch of my father's other family and how, if things had been different, this could have been Norma's house.

Test the Air

HENRY AND I WATCHED OUR CHANGE trickle into the glass case, and as the bus pulled away we followed Della toward the back. She sat next to a thin, gray-haired Negro woman in a maid's uniform. Della never wore a uniform— one of the many reasons I didn't think of her as the maid. Della was less a keeper of the house than a keeper of the family.

She sat us in an empty seat behind her. I let Henry have the window, knowing that if I didn't, he would make a stink. Henry had an artful way of making a stink, especially in public, that made me appear selfish and brutish while he came off as innocent and above the fray.

"I have to talk to Santa Claus." Henry stared out over the neighborhood, looking worried. He was dressed in Mitchell's red winter coat and floppy-eared hat.

"Santa Claus doesn't come till the end of the parade." I looked up the aisle. Most of the passengers were Negroes except for a lone white woman who sat up front, talking to the driver. It was still the law in Greenville in 1963 that Negroes sat in the back, filling seats toward the front, and that whites sat in the front, filling seats toward the back, and if there were not enough seats for whites, then Negroes had to stand.

"I hope he got my list." Henry had mailed his Christmas list to Santa Claus in early August, believing Santa was impressed by promptness.

Della opened her big pocketbook and took out a pack of gum. She offered the other woman a piece. Then she gave a piece each to Henry and me. Chewing, we pressed our noses against the cold bus window, watching the neighborhood pass, but from a much higher angle than usual. The maids and the yardmen talked and laughed across the aisle. Riding the bus with Della was like being levitated to a slightly higher, more social realm.

I stared out the window, thinking about what had happened at school that morning. When we returned to school after Thanksgiving, we found a new teacher. Miss Hawkins had retired and gone to live with a cousin in North Carolina, or at least that is what we were told. At first, the mood of the class was jubilant. But after two weeks, the bump on Norma's forehead disappeared, Mr. Keener stopped dropping by our classroom so often, and we returned to geography, long division, and spelling. Mrs. Watts was a young red-haired woman who, whenever one of us misspelled a word, would shake her head and press her hand to her forehead in mock despair.

The most difficult aspect of school for me was Norma. Ever since we had taken her home from Dr. Norton's office, my feelings toward her had gradually changed. Somehow our roles had reversed. Now when I tried to talk to her, she buried her head in a book or got up to sharpen her pencil.

On this particular day at recess, when I saw her walk across the playground, I had made up my mind to speak to her. I called to her, but she didn't even glance my way, so I walked after her. The faster I walked, the faster she walked. She started to run. I ran after her, following her past the monkey bars into the woods, until I cornered her by the fence.

She kept her back to me, staring through the chain links at the street.

"How come you won't talk to me?" I said, catching my breath.

"Turnabout is fair play," she said stuffing her hands in her coat pockets, her breath visible in the December air. Her coat looked new but was a size too big; her mother probably had gotten a deal on it.

"You're getting me back?" I asked, hearing the edge in my voice.

Norma laced her fingers through the fence and rattled it like she wanted out.

"I believe you are my sister," I said.

Norma slowly faced me. "Half sister," she said, emphasizing the "half." "You haven't told him about me, have you?"

I shook my head. "Why didn't you tell him when you had the chance?"

She picked up a stick and began running it back and forth across the fence. "My mother said it was up to me if I wanted to tell him."

"You told *me.*"

"And look what happened," she said, pointing the stick at me. "You stopped talking to me." She sat down on a log.

"Does your mother know you told me?"

"I told her you were the kind of boy who keeps things to himself. And she said, 'Like father, like son.' "

I sat beside her. I was in over my head, but then I often felt that way around Norma. I had never thought of myself as being any more closemouthed than anyone else.

Across the playground, swings creaked, the slide popped in the cold, and several boys piled onto one side of the see-saw, hoisting Billy Bukowski into the air.

"My father has been trying to find you," I said.

"Nanna told us he has been writing her," she said.

"Your grandmother lives in Wilmington, right?"

She looked at me, surprised.

"My father would want to know you are who you are," I said, crumbling a leaf.

"It's not up to him," she said, digging the heels of her saddle oxfords into the ground. "It's up to me, if and when I tell him." She shook her stick at me. "You better not say a word."

As soon as she said this, I felt freed up in a curious way. Some part of me had believed all along that she had revealed who she was to me so I would eventually tell my father. I had thought she had deliberately put me in the position of reluctant messenger. Now it seemed that she had told me simply because she wanted me to know.

The recess bell rang, and children ran toward the building, forming a line behind Mrs. Watts. Norma and I sat there, watching the children file into the school.

"Why don't you meet me at the parade?" I asked. "We'll be in front of the Krispy Kreme." Then, thinking she might be worried about seeing my father, I added, "He won't be there. He never goes."

"I can't come meet you some place like a friend would," she said, tossing the stick down.

"How come?"

"Because I have changed us," she said, standing up. "I have made us related."

"You didn't *make* us related," I said. But she was already sprinting across the playground, her big coat lifting up behind her.

A POLICEMAN STOOD IN FRONT of his squad car, rerouting traffic around Main Street through back streets. The bus passed Springwood, the big downtown cemetery— acres and acres of memorials.

"There it is." Henry tapped the window, as always never missing a chance to point out the cemetery where Mitchell was buried. He hadn't attended Mitchell's funeral because our parents thought he was too young, but he had pumped me for details, down to exactly how they lowered the coffin into the ground.

"We'll be buried there too someday." Henry said this cheerfully, as if it were something to look forward to.

We passed the back entrances to Ivey's, JCPenney, the Carolina Theater, and the Ottaray Hotel. It was several minutes before we pulled up in front of the Dollar Store— an ancient, wooden building whose three floors offered great mounds of cheap fabric and musty discount clothes, some of which had been buried in the bins for so long that the material had faded or the buttons yellowed. Everyone in town shopped at the Dollar Store, but poor whites and Negroes had to buy their clothes here, unable to afford the pricier department stores down the street.

After the bus doors folded open and we climbed down, Della took our hands and headed us past the Dollar Store and down Main Street. Downtown was already busy with families staking out their six feet of curb. Office workers hung out of their windows, waving. Sober-faced patrol boys and Boy Scouts lined both sides of the street, charged with keeping the crowd behind yellow ropes. The city had hung the same ragged lights and tinsel they had been hanging for twenty years.

Downtown always reminded me of being with Aunt Louise and Uncle Clem before Mitchell's death. Sometimes, on Saturday afternoons, Uncle Clem used to drive Louise, Mitchell, and me downtown. We ate chicken and dumplings at the S&W Cafeteria, stopped at Woolworth's to admire the aquariums so packed with goldfish that they glowed, then walked up the street to the Fox Theater to see who John Wayne was saving this week.

We were a block from my mother's office when a grizzled Negro man stepped up to us, holding his hand out to Della. "Spare a dime, miss?" He clutched a worn overcoat around him, his hand shaking. His breath reeked of beer. Henry and I pulled back, but Della opened her purse and dropped two dimes in the old man's hand.

As we walked on down the street, I kept looking over my shoulder at the man, who was already approaching someone else. "Uncle Clem says some Negroes are just no-'count." As soon as I said it, I knew that I had made a mistake.

Della froze. She cocked her head and looked at me. She leaned over and for a moment I thought she might slap me. "You tell Mr. Clem," she said in a very slow way, "that us coloreds don't have the corner on no-'count."

It was the only time that I had ever seen Della get truly angry about something I said. The intensity of her reaction threw me. After all, I was only repeating what someone else had said. I felt like I had dissolved our history together, and for a matter of excruciating minutes, we became complete strangers.

Her eyes shining with what I realized were tears, she buttoned the top button of my coat. As she walked Henry and me toward our mother's office, there was a new stiffness in the way she held our hands.

WE FOUND MY MOTHER AT HER DESK in the newsroom, typing. She was so big now that she had to sit back. I thought of typing as a fatherly activity, so it was always an adjustment to see my mother at her desk, her hands flying across the keys.

I liked the newsroom din—reporters, almost all of them men, hunched over their typewriters, typing as if their lives depended on it, creating a magnificent clatter. I was impressed how they typed while talking on the phone or shouting a question to a colleague. This was the Olympics of typing, and these reporters were all sprinters. I knew that none of them, including my mother, could match my father for overall endurance.

"Have a seat, Della." My mother pulled around a couple of chairs from empty desks, then sat back down. "I'm on deadline." My mother began typing again, while she read from the yellow notepad beside the typewriter. "There's coffee if you want to warm up." She gestured to the other side of the busy newsroom to a coffeepot on a little table.

"That's all right." Della folded her hands across her pocketbook.

I rolled a sheet of paper into a typewriter at an empty desk and began tapping out words with one finger. I could hear the rumble of the presses in the basement, and the whole building trembled.

I saw Della look up from the newspaper she was reading and gaze in the direction of the coffeepot. She seemed to want coffee but for some reason was hesitant. It didn't occur to me that she might not be up to crossing a roomful of busy white people, but I sensed a chance to make up. I walked through the maze of desks, poured her a cup, and then carried the coffee back across the room to her as an offering. She sipped the coffee, then smiled for the first time since my remark.

My mother ripped a page out of her typewriter, scooped up the other pages she had typed, and hurried into one of the glassed-in offices. We could see through the window that she dropped the story onto an editor's desk. The editor was a small man with a green eyeshade. He asked her something. She pointed out the window to us, waiting. He raised his hand as if to indicate he understood.

It might have been our recent late-night talks about the newsroom or noticing my mother's name on stories in the paper or overhearing people in the bakery or at the Eight O'Clock Superette compliment her on a piece she had written. All I know is that seeing my mother in action at her place of work had begun to give me the same kind of inner tingle that I got while reading a biography about Betsy Ross or Annie Oakley.

We walked down the sidewalk with Henry and me in front and my mother and Della behind. We pushed through the crowd, passing the Belk department store, the old courthouse, and the Jack Tar Poinsett Hotel. When we arrived at the Krispy Kreme, Beverly and Leigh weren't there. It was an annual tradition that we meet Della's daughter and her mother in front of the doughnut shop. But since the parade hadn't started, we stood outside and ate warm, sticky doughnuts that melted in our mouths and crusted our fingers with sugar.

Della stood on the steps of the Krispy Kreme, looking over the crowd. "It ain't like Beverly to be late."

Henry and I squeezed our way to the curb as three motorcycle cops rumbled past, followed by shivering bare-thighed majorettes holding a banner between them. Behind the majorettes, the Greenville High School band, in red uniforms and tall hats, marked an uneven time. The drum major raised his baton, and eventually the band members all raised their instruments to their lips and blew. What started out as "O Come All Ye Faithful" quickly disintegrated into an atonal symphony.

The first float, a flatbed pulled by a pickup, was the Shriner's Children Hospital float—pale, fragile-looking children in wheelchairs and on crutches, waving too vigorously. The float was escorted by Shriners—middle-aged men in fezzes and gold jackets, weaving miniature cars in and out of the line. A flatbed of shivering beauty queens passed, pressing their crowns to their heads—Miss Greenville, Miss Spartanburg, Miss Anderson, Miss Fountain Inn, and Miss Traveler's Rest.

A cheer went up as the band from Greenville's Negro high school, Sterling High, marched down Main Street. The bass drum kept fast, lively time, and the band members shuffled forward and then rocked back on their heels in unison, dancing with their instruments. When the drum major, a tall, angular boy, pumped his arms and blew his whistle, the band played. The music hung together, filling downtown with heartfelt strains of "O Little Town of Bethlehem."

It wasn't long before Leigh arrived. She was a short, stout woman who wore the same square-heeled lace-up shoes my Aunt Louise wore. She had helped raise my mother and Uncle Charlie, but she also baby-sat for us, bringing us paper sacks of Moon Pies and pork rinds.

Leigh said Beverly had decided to go to the parade with other school friends. Della was upset, saying that this was a tradition, that Beverly could be with her girlfriends anytime. When we were little, Beverly had come to our house with Della and we would play all afternoon. But as soon as we started school, we weren't allowed to play together. And at last year's parade, we had stood on the curb, embarrassed that we no longer knew each other.

"Not that long ago we stand out here with your mama, Miss Muriel." Leigh bit into a chocolate doughnut. "You and Mr. Charlie and Della." She looked down at my mother's stomach. "Della tell me the baby been kicking."

"He's getting impatient." My mother touched her stomach.

"You carrying it high." Leigh swallowed the last of her doughnut. "It be a girl."

"Mama, you told me Beverly was going to be a boy," Della said.

"Might as well, the way she climb trees and wrestle the boys."

"Don't pay Mama no mind," Della said to my mother.

Leigh gave an indignant grunt. "Miss Muriel carrying that baby like her mama carried her and the other baby girl . . ." She looked at my mother as if she realized too late what she had said. That other baby girl had died along with my grandmother. They were also buried in Springwood, the baby's miniature headstone next to my grandmother's.

Henry stood on the curb eating another doughnut and watching the parade intently. I tried to look interested in the parade so the women wouldn't notice me and change the subject.

"I have always wondered," I heard my mother say, "weren't you in the room when my mother died?"

"Yes'm." Leigh wound her scarf around her neck.

"Did you speak to her?"

Leigh sipped her coffee and looked off in the distance as if trying to remember. "I come in to change the sheets again. Your mama's eyes be closed. I thought she was sleeping. She lost so much blood. Your daddy sit up all night. Your mama's Aunt Louise come in that morning to spell him." Leigh took another sip of her coffee. "Miss Louise went to the door to talk to the doctor. That's when your mama open her eyes a little and ask me about the baby. Course, the baby be dead by then but I tell her it sleeping in the cradle. I wasn't sure she hear me. She close her eyes and never wake up." Leigh shivered and pulled her coat around her. "I always wonder if I do the right thing, lying like that to your mama."

"Of course you did." My mother put her hand on Leigh's shoulder.

"She died content," Della said.

"What she think when she get to Heaven and find the little baby already waiting for her?" Leigh sighed. "That baby an angel sent to lead your mama home."

I examined the bulge of my mother's overcoat. Was that

what this baby was? An angel come to lead my mother away? And in the middle of all this, someone took my hand. Norma put her finger to her lips, nodding toward my mother, who was caught up in her conversation with Leigh. She pressed something into my hands. A wrapped present. "Merry Christmas, Jeru," she whispered. She smiled at Henry and disappeared into the crowd.

"Was that your girlfriend?" asked Henry, watching a passing float with Cub Scouts pretending to warm themselves around a papier-mâché fire. Henry's tone wasn't accusative, just interested.

I stared off in the direction Norma had disappeared.

"What did she give you?" Henry asked.

I unwrapped the paper. It was a new copy of *John F. Kennedy and PT-109.* I opened the cover. On the flyleaf she had written, "Now you don't have to check it out anymore. Norma."

THE NEXT SATURDAY MORNING my mother and Henry took me to Aunt Louise's, where we were all going to have lunch and I was going to spend the night. We left my father writing in the basement. The first thing I noticed when we pulled up to Aunt Louise's was the "For Sale" sign in the front yard. I had hated the sign since the afternoon two weeks earlier when a suited man in a shiny car pulled up and without asking anybody stabbed it in the yard and drove off. Uncle Clem had pulled the sign up and tossed it into the hedge. Aunt Louise, who had made the decision to put the house on the market, made him replace it.

Aunt Louise wasn't in the kitchen when we walked in, though beans were boiling and chicken was sizzling in the frying pan. The table was set for five. We walked through the whole house. We found a few half-packed boxes. My mother and Aunt Louise had set the date of their moving into Autumn Care as the middle of February, so that, among other reasons, the family could have one last Christmas on Howe Street. Aunt Louise said they were moving even if the house didn't sell. Clem would not discuss it.

The upstairs bedrooms were empty as well. My mother began to look worried. We heard the front door shut. We found them in the kitchen where Clem was putting his toolbox away and Louise was taking the chicken off the stove. Louise wasn't using her cane. As soon as the moving date had been set, her hip improved.

"Well, there you are." Louise set the pieces of chicken on paper towels. She said they had been next door at Mary Moore's. "Mary asked Clem to change some washers." Aunt Louise turned the burners down. "I went with him to make sure he wasn't rude."

Clem opened his toolbox and put away two wrenches. "I wanted Louise with me for protection."

"Muriel? Are you all right?" Aunt Louise was looking at my mother, who had sat down at the kitchen table. She didn't appear upset to me. She wasn't crying. Her eyes weren't even red.

"What is it?" Louise put her arm on my mother's shoulder. My mother shrugged. Aunt Louise frowned at Clem.

"Did I do something?" he asked.

Louise shooed us out of the kitchen. "Brother, you and the boys go play. Lunch won't be for a little while yet."

Henry and I followed Clem into the other room. I said I had to go to the bathroom, so I went into the hall and tiptoed past the bathroom and stood at the other kitchen door. I spent a large part of my childhood on the other side of doors or just around corners. Eavesdropping on adults was a survival tactic, since an adult, by definition, was someone who kept things from children.

"What is it?" Aunt Louise spooned instant coffee into a couple of cups, then poured hot water from a kettle on the stove. She set one cup in front of my mother and sat down across from her.

"When I walked into this house and you weren't here . . ." My mother rubbed her forehead. "It hit me. In a little while you won't be in this house at all."

"It's time." Aunt Louise sipped her coffee.

"Maybe we should try to find another housekeeper." My mother warmed her hands on the cup. "She could live up-stairs. Maybe we could find a white one so Clem wouldn't offend her. I don't want you to leave. I grew up in this house. I need you in this house."

"It has gotten to be too much." Aunt Louise looked around the kitchen, which was the brightest room in the house, with the wide window at the nook that looked out over the drive and two more windows at the sink that faced the backyard. But it was the floor I had always no-ticed: the ancient linoleum had been worn into dark paths connecting the old gas stove, the rusted refrigerator, and the ceramic sink, chipped and stained from generations of dishwashing.

My mother sighed. "But you and Clem in this house are my last connection. To Mama. To Daddy. To Aunt Lucille. Aunt Valma. I even feel Mitchell here more than any-where." She set her spoon on the saucer with a clink. She spread her hand on her stomach. "It breaks my heart to think this child won't grow up to drink coffee at this table." She took Aunt Louise's hand. Off in the other room, I heard dice rattle in a tin cup, which meant Uncle Clem and Henry were already playing Parcheesi.

Aunt Louise got up to check the beans, then opened the oven and looked at the biscuits. "We met Leigh at the parade the other night," my mother said, sipping her coffee.

"How is she?"

"She told me Mama died thinking the baby was alive."

"It's true." Louise slid the biscuits out and set them on top of the oven. "I'm just glad your mother didn't ask me. I wouldn't have had Leigh's presence of mind."

"Leigh said she thought the baby was an angel. Do you believe in angels?" my mother asked.

I nearly jumped out of my skin when I realized Uncle Clem was standing behind me, peeking into the kitchen, too. "What you up to, boy?" he whispered. "You looking a little pale. You been listening in on them? What were they jabbering about? Nursing home? Don't pay no mind to those hens." He led me down the hall, past the glass case of cups and teapots. "Ain't a good idea to listen in on women. They don't talk like you and me talk, to tell each other things."

"They don't?"

"They talk to see how something sounds. I wouldn't call it lying, but it ain't the truth as we know it. Women talk to test the air."

In the den, Henry sat on one side of the card table, holding Clem's cow horn to his ear. "Everything sounds like one big echo," he said.

Uncle Clem scooted over on his cot, while I sat in a chair across from Henry. The Parcheesi board, yellowed with decades of tea and coffee stains, was open in the middle of the card table. The little colored disks, what we called "men," had been worn smooth by generations of children Uncle Clem had taught to play. My mother, my uncle, my grandmother, even my great-grandmother had rolled these same dice and slid these same men along the cross-shaped path that eventually led home.

When Aunt Louise called us to lunch, we left the game as it was so that we could finish after we ate. We followed Uncle Clem into the kitchen and found my mother setting the table. We sat down with my mother and Aunt Louise to a big meal of fried chicken, green beans, biscuits, and iced tea.

Aunt Louise gave the blessing. "Lord, we ask you to guide Lyndon Johnson in his new job as president. Help us feed and heat all the shut-ins . . ."

"Whoa." My mother laughed. We raised our heads. "This baby's really kicking," she said, holding herself.

Aunt Louise came around and put her hand on my mother's belly. Uncle Clem got up, too, as did Henry and I. It was an eerie moment, like a seance, all of us crowded around her, our hands on her stomach, waiting for a signal from the other world.

"I feel like a melon at the Eight O'Clock," my mother said.

"There," Aunt Louise whispered. "He kicked."

"I don't feel nothing," Uncle Clem said, sitting back down.

"I felt it," said Henry excitedly. He bent down even with

her stomach and, cupping his hands around his mouth, called out, "Hello in there." Then he pressed his ear against her stomach.

I sat back down. I had felt something all right—the unmistakable flutter of wings.

CHAPTER EIGHT

Run Away

THE AFTERNOON I BURNED MY FATHER'S MANUSCRIPT
had started innocently enough. It was Christmas Eve and I
had climbed high in the magnolia tree. I always climbed
higher than Mitchell or Roger had ever dared. Heights did
not bother me. In fact, climbing trees was the closest I
came to athletic prowess.

From this perspective, I could see houses and yards all
around, making my neighborhood feel more like a whole
place, like the village on Roger's train track, the one Dr.
Avant set up in their living room every Christmas. It
wasn't the same crammed in his apartment's empty dining
room, windowless with faded carpet. Last week, Roger
and I had gone over to play with the train. Dr. Avant fed us
tuna-fish sandwiches on a card table and let us watch
White Christmas on his little black-and-white set. We had
helped him assemble an artificial tree and hung satiny red
balls he had bought on sale at the Lewis Plaza Pharmacy.
It was sad, and I would not have stayed had it not been for
the bewildered look on Roger's face.

I climbed a limb higher. It was a cold, gray afternoon.

The sky was weighted with clouds, and the weatherman predicted sleet, maybe even a little snow—a rare occurrence in Greenville.

My mother and Henry had gone to deliver Della's presents. My mother had come outside and called for me, looking everywhere but up. I hadn't intended to hide, but when she began calling, I didn't answer. As I sat up in the magnolia and watched her walk around the yard calling my name, I had the sensation that this was what it was like to be dead—calmly observing from above, slightly amused at the urgency of the living down below.

My mother had probably assumed Roger and I had ridden down to Reedy River or were meandering through the neighborhood on our bikes. Often during the Christmas holidays, we disappeared for entire afternoons. But Roger was at his father's apartment again, this time with his sister and brothers. The children were spending Christmas Eve with Dr. Avant and Christmas Day with their mother. Roger had been at a real loss lately, not sure how to go about portioning himself out.

I climbed down, stepping on the dead magnolia leaves that collected at the base of the tree. That sound, the hollow crackle, always reminded me of Mitchell. It was the one way I knew he was under here, if I was outside the tree.

I had come down because no one was home. My father had gone to the Christmas staff party his old ad agency held each year. His boss had called the previous night during supper to invite him. After my father got off the phone and came back to the table, my mother said she thought it was a good sign that his boss had called. "They still want you," she said.

"Which is why I'm not going." My father sat at the table, staring at his buttered potato, his face gaunt and dark from not shaving. His hair looked as if it hadn't been combed in weeks. He had spent more time in the basement, sometimes not even coming upstairs for meals. His eyes remained bloodshot. He smoked so many cigarettes that a cloud trailed him from room to room.

"We have been over this." My mother put down her fork. "We agreed you would work on the book one year and then go back to work."

My father smoothed his folded napkin on the table. "I can't write ad copy anymore. I can't be clever anymore." He glanced in our direction, embarrassed to be discussing this in front of his children.

"My salary isn't enough," my mother said.

"We have been doing all right."

"We dip into savings every month. Pretty soon there won't be anything left. We can't even afford decent Christmas presents."

"For years I have put Erector sets and Play-Doh factories before my writing," he said. One of the cats jumped into my father's lap, and my father dropped him back down.

"At least Santa pays for ours," Henry said, spooning up a bite of fruit cocktail. I sat across from my father, eating a dinner roll and wondering if he might leave us.

"A few more months." My father held out his hands to my mother.

"We don't have a few months."

"And whose fault is that?"

"No one's. It is a divine gift." She lowered her voice. "However, I seem to recall some rather passionate cooperation." My mother leaned back in her chair.

My father blushed.

"I believe in you," my mother said. "I believe in your book. I believe it must be a beautiful book." This was the first time I realized that my mother hadn't read my father's book either.

My father crumpled his napkin. "For all your talk about spirit, you are still mired in the world."

"I'm mired in family," she said. "This family comes first."

My father leaned over the table. "Then why aren't you having a C-section?"

My mother blanched at this.

My father started to eat his potato but then pushed his chair back. He disappeared down the hallway, closing the basement door behind him. He didn't start typing for a long time.

I OPENED THE DOOR SLOWLY and stepped inside, kicking my way through balled-up typewriter paper to my father's desk, noticing the careful stack of pages that was the manuscript. I had decided to sneak into my father's office, which I did now and then, to practice typing.

I sat in his chair, rolled a clean sheet of paper into his typewriter, placed my fingers on the keys, and, taking a deep breath, began to type as fast as I could. I made the same clatter that my father made, and when I pushed the carriage back, it rang just as it did for him. But when I looked up, I saw I had typed lines of gibberish—with letters, numbers, and various punctuation all mixed together. Still I kept typing, thrilled to be making the right sounds, until I hit too many keys and jammed it. I pried the keys apart, then pulled the sheet of gibberish out of the typewriter and buried it in the trash can.

I was on my way out of his office when my eye fell on a stack of magazines on a bottom bookshelf. This was the other reason I sometimes sneaked down here. I picked one up. I flipped through the slick pages, my fingers traced the heavy breasts of women who slid their hands down their bare thighs, licking their lips. I flipped through another magazine and then another. I felt a pleasing hardness below my belt. I looked up and saw all the women on the office walls watching me. I recalled something my mother had read to me from Mary Baker Eddy when she was trying to get me to eat fewer Pinwheel cookies. " 'If we look to the body for pleasure, we find pain . . . ' "

I was upset with myself for succumbing to these magazines and upset with my father for having them in temptation's way. I noticed a book of matches beside the typewriter. With my heart pounding, I carried the magazines into the backyard and piled them in the middle of the drive. I remembered his sketches, which felt like a roomful of witnesses. I tore them all down and piled them in the driveway, too.

I should have stopped there, and would have, if it had not been for the fire itself, which had transported me with its crackle and its heat to some clean, purged place. I went back into his office and before I knew what I had done, I carried the manuscript outside and dangled one typewritten sheet over the flames, then another and another.

The smoke burned my eyes. Ashes with a typed phrase or two floated above the drive, settling across the backyard like singed fortunes. All around me, the leaves began to jump, sounding like the scratchings of invisible birds. Sleet bounced off my jacket. I don't know how long I had stood there when a car door slammed out on the street. I ran inside, shutting my father's office door, and raced up the basement stairs in time to meet my mother in the kitchen.

Inside, Henry was at the back window. It was sleeting heavier, the ice ticking against the glass. I joined him and watched the flames just barely flickering in the driveway.

"What is that down there?" he whispered, knowing it was something to whisper about.

"You don't want to know."

"If you don't tell me . . ." He raised his voice, looking off in the direction of the kitchen and our mother.

"I burned some stuff," I whispered in his ear.

"Whose stuff?"

"Daddy's."

His eyes widened. "You didn't?"

I saw what an unspeakable thing I had done reflected in Henry's expression.

"Run away." He looked at the smear in the driveway.

When my father arrived home, Henry and I were in the front room, playing Booby Trap by the light of the Christmas tree. Booby Trap was a tense little game with small red and blue wooden disks that we tried to remove gingerly without setting off the spring trap. Henry had suggested we play something to get my mind off my troubles. He had even gotten up in the middle of the game and brought me a Fig Newton like a jailer brings a prisoner his last meal.

I had set off the trap, and little disks clattered everywhere as the front door opened and our father, speckled with snow, walked into the living room and stood there looking around as if uncertain he was in the right house.

My mother came in from the kitchen, wiping her hands on her apron. "I was beginning to worry."

"The streets are bad." He still stood there, looking bewildered, his coat dripping.

"How did it go?" My mother helped him take off his coat.

My father walked over to the window and looked out at the falling snow.

"How was the party?" My mother hung his coat on the stand by the door. Henry and I looked at each other, both of us wondering if somehow he already knew about the burned manuscript. I checked for the quickest escape route.

"The party was okay." He continued to stare out at the snow.

"What's wrong?" My mother stepped up beside him.

My father rubbed his eyes. "They offered me my old job." He turned to her. "I had every intention of turning them down." My father picked up a Hershey's Kiss from a candy dish on the coffee table and slowly unwrapped it. "But I accepted." He popped the chocolate into his mouth. "They're giving me a raise."

My mother laughed. "A raise for quitting." She kissed him. I hadn't seen her so happy since before Mitchell's death. "When do you start?"

"The first of February." He sat on the couch.

She sat beside him, putting her arm around him. "That's my due date."

"I should be finished with my book by then," he said to himself. "If I work very hard." He pushed himself up off the couch, headed for the basement door.

Henry looked at me, panic in his eyes.

As my father started to open the basement door, I ran

over and planted myself in front of it. "You can't go down there."

My father gripped the doorknob. "And why not?"

"You just can't." I spread my arms against the door.

"What's going on?" My father started to pull me out of the way.

I held on to the doorknob.

"I know what the boy means." My mother came up beside me. "It's Christmas Eve. He wants you to spend time with us."

My father frowned. "You're right. I won't work tonight." He opened the door. "There are a few things I need to take care of. Shouldn't take long."

I slammed the door shut. "You can't."

"Jeru is right," my mother said. "If you go down there, we won't see you for three or four hours."

"All right." He raised his hands. "I won't set foot in my office until after Christmas."

"Come help me with the hot chocolate." My mother led my father by the hand.

I didn't move from the basement door until my father had disappeared into the kitchen with my mother. I sank back on the couch. Henry wiped pretend sweat from his forehead.

"I can't keep him away from his office forever," I said.

My mother and father came out of the kitchen. My father was carrying a tray with hot chocolate and butter cookies Mrs. Avant had brought over. He set the tray on the coffee table. Then he put a Christmas record on the hi-fi, and the four of us sat on the couch, sipped hot chocolate, and admired the Christmas tree, while Perry Como crooned "O Little Town of Bethlehem."

"You have had a healing. That's what has happened here." My mother snuggled against my father, attempted to pull her legs up under her, then gave up.

Henry sat next to me, eating a cookie and squinting at the Christmas tree in the way our father had taught us, making everything appear fuzzy and Christmas-cardish. I couldn't bring myself to squint at the tree as Perry Como sang, "The hopes and fears of all the years/Are met in thee tonight."

"Our second Christmas without him," my mother said.

My father set his cup on the coffee table. "Sometimes I think I'll find him in his room working one of those jigsaw puzzles he spent hours on."

"He is still with us," my mother said and covered my father's hand with her own. "Death is the lie of life." She was quoting Mary Baker Eddy. I could tell by the way she didn't sound like herself.

CHAPTER NINE

From the Ground Up

FOLLOWING CLEM UP THE BACK STAIRS from the wood-pile beside the toolshed, I carried three pieces of split poplar. We stomped the snow off our feet and passed through the kitchen, where my mother and Aunt Leila washed and stacked the dishes from Christmas lunch. The rich smell of turkey filled the house.

"You must be happy that he's going back," said Aunt Leila in her extravagant up-country accent. She was a slender woman, and her high heels and tight-fitting dresses were not nearly as sexy as her low, steamy voice, which wrapped itself around words like wisteria. She dried the big turkey platter and put it away.

"It does make things easier." My mother, up to her elbows in soapsuds, stood at the sink, rinsing plates and setting them in the drain.

"Of course it does." She lowered her voice. "I know losing a son is hard for a father." She blew smoke toward the dining room. "But it's time Warren got out of that basement and rejoined the human race."

I didn't hear my mother's response as Clem and I went

through to the dining room, where Uncle Charlie and my father were dismantling the table. Uncle Charlie was a kindhearted man whose deadpan expression never gave any hint of emotion. Aunt Leila said it came from fifteen years of practicing law. "If you're married to a lawyer," she would say, filing her fingernails or checking her lipstick in her compact, "the jury is always out."

I didn't know what they had been discussing, but I could see my father's ironic smile, a sure sign he was detouring into the mystical.

"It is a disciplined communion with an inner world." My father's eyes lit up, as he helped Uncle Charlie pull the extra leaves out of the middle of the table. "A frame of reference," he said as they shoved the table back together.

Uncle Charlie frowned, the way I had seen friends and relatives frown whenever my father brought up spirituality. It wasn't a frown of disapproval but of puzzlement. One moment they had been having a perfectly normal conversation with this perfectly normal fellow, the next moment they found themselves collared by a zealot.

I followed Clem to the living room, where he already had a fire going in the fireplace. Christmas was the only time Clem and Louise opened up the living room. The rest of the year it sat cold and unoccupied. Years before, it had been a gathering place for the students and professors whom my aunt occasionally boarded. There was even a hi-fi and a cabinet full of seventy-eights a professor had left.

But ever since the college had moved and the boarders with it, no one ever went in the living room except me. I liked its lonely mustiness and spent many afternoons in the window seat or in one of the great stuffed chairs, reading a school biography or thumbing through my aunt's illustrated set of Dickens.

I dropped my firewood beside Clem's on the hearth. Clem pulled back the fire screen and set more wood on the fire. It hissed and sizzled. "We might as well burn it all. Eh, Jaybird?" He brushed snow from the brim of his cap. He unzipped his jacket and threw it across a chair. "Last fire we'll burn in this house," he said over his shoulder. It was the only reference anyone had made all day to this being our final Christmas there. Aunt Louise had found a buyer.

Henry was on the rug with our two girl cousins who were playing house with their dolls in a fort Henry had constructed from Lincoln Logs. I stood beside Uncle Clem, feeling the heat of the fire against my pants. I smelled that Aunt Louise had started a pot of coffee. She would have set the cakes out on the kitchen table by now.

"I don't want you to go," I said to Uncle Clem, tossing a ball of wrapping paper onto the fire, which transformed in my mind into a typewritten page of my father's novel.

Clem put his hand on my shoulder.

Outside, the snow dripped from the front porch. It had snowed four inches—a Christmas record, the paper said. Even so, it wasn't enough snow for me. My heart sank when I saw the sun glitter through the clouds. I had hoped once we had gotten to Aunt Louise's that a blizzard would sock us in, keeping us away from Afton Avenue and the inevitable consequences of what I had done.

It was nearly dark and the melting snow had turned to a

sheet of ice when Louise and Clem walked us to our cars. Across the street, the outlines of the old college buildings were etched in snow. We carried warm plates and casserole dishes covered with aluminum foil, setting them on the car floors.

"Careful, Louise." Uncle Charlie took her arm. He and my father had taken turns clearing the walk with a shovel I had fetched from the toolshed.

Aunt Leila kissed my cheek as I was studying the pinched head of a glass-eyed fox that hung from her fur.

"Merry Christmas, Unc," Uncle Charlie said, clapping Clem on the back.

"Same to ya," Uncle Clem said under his breath before spitting tobacco and staining the snow. Without another word, he limped toward the house.

"Poor Uncle Clem," Aunt Leila said, watching him go in.

"Don't worry about that old coot," Aunt Louise said.

Aunt Leila took Louise's hand. "I can't believe that this is actually the last Christmas on Howe Street. Somehow the snow seems fitting."

"Leila, don't be so maudlin." Uncle Charlie rubbed his forehead and looked away.

"Honestly," Aunt Louise said, "I'm more relieved than you will ever know."

We stood on the sidewalk, the adults looking back at the house. A small white "Sale Pending" sign had been pasted across the "For Sale" sign. I stared across the frozen campus where a lone Negro boy pulled his sled. The adults elaborated on their good-byes, not saying much of anything the way only adults can. They seemed reluctant to leave, and for once I wished they would never stop talking.

Uncle Charlie and his family drove off, and then my mother walked Aunt Louise into the house while my father, Henry, and I got in the car. When my mother came back, she said Clem hadn't spoken a word to her and that Louise seemed exhausted. My father started to drive away. My mother kept her eye on their house as we rounded the campus.

"They seem so alone," my mother said.

"Maybe I should spend the night," I heard myself say.

My mother turned around in her seat. "Don't you want to get home and play with your presents?"

"I can play with them later," I said, trying to sound as if it were a tough decision.

My mother looked at my father. "It might be good." My father circled back around the campus and pulled in front of the house. Henry watched me, openmouthed.

My mother caught my arm as I hopped out. "What will you sleep in?"

"Uncle Clem has some nightshirts."

"Wave if it's all right," my father called.

I found Aunt Louise in the kitchen. She said it was fine, so I ran out on the porch and waved them on, still unable to believe my luck. Of course my father would find out tonight, but I wouldn't be there. He might call or, if he was upset enough, he might come get me.

Uncle Clem sat in the front room, staring at the fire. "I built this house from the foundation up." He stood, took the poker, and jabbed at the glowing logs. "Hired a brick mason to build the chimney, an old-timer and his son. They bought the bricks from the college, left over from one of the classrooms. Bricks made by slaves." He tapped the bricks with his poker.

At supper we sat in the little nook, eating leftovers. After he had finished his soup, Uncle Clem poured himself a glass of buttermilk and crumbled corn bread into it, spooning soggy bites into his mouth. After a few minutes of silence, Aunt Louise said, "Don't take it so hard, Little Brother."

Uncle Clem pushed himself up from the table, took his cap and his jacket down off the rack by the back door.

"Where do you think you're going?" Aunt Louise looked up at Clem.

"To get more wood."

"Everybody has gone home."

He tugged open the back door. A blast of cold air made us shiver. "That fire ain't going out." We could hear Clem slowly make his way down the stairs, the house trembling with each step. Aunt Louise told me to put on my coat and follow him to make sure he didn't fall. I caught up with him in the garden, past the raised beds that looked like graves in the snow. The snow squeaked underneath our feet. The vague whiteness of the ground made the night itself appear darker. I had a sudden image of my father on his knees in our drive, sifting ashes through his fingers.

When we reached the woodpile, all we could see were shadows. Uncle Clem threw back the piece of canvas he used to keep the wood dry. He loaded my arms, then dug into the pile and lifted several pieces himself. Something slowly shifted in his arms. He dropped the wood but something was wrapped around his arm. "Goddamn!" He tried to shake it off, but it wouldn't let go. Finally, he flung it off, and it landed with a wet plop in the snow and slowly slithered away. He was shaking his wrist.

"Goddamn! It bit me! Feels like hot needles." He held up his wrist. "Let's get this wood in." He picked up a couple of pieces, and we climbed the back stairs. As we walked into the light of the kitchen, Uncle Clem said calmly, "Sis, I been bit."

Aunt Louise came over, wiping her hands on a dish towel.

"A snake was in the woodpile," I said.

"I reckon I woke him." Clem glanced at his wrist.

"We better call the doctor," Louise said, looking at the bite.

"No need." Clem turned away. "It just stings a little." I followed him to the front room, where we set the wood beside the hearth. We could hear Aunt Louise dialing the phone. She came into the living room, where Uncle Clem was down on one knee feeding the fire.

"The phone's out," she said. "Jeru, run next door and see if Mary Moore's phone is working." She held out her hand. "No, wait. Mary has gone to her sister's."

"They ain't no need for all this," Clem said as we followed him into the den, where he turned on the television to watch Huntley and Brinkley and sat down on his cot. "Ain't no worse than a bee sting." Uncle Clem held out his wrist, showing two small marks. He waved Aunt Louise out of the way of the television. "You been drinking muddy water, Sis."

"Clem, you know better than to dig around in that old woodpile at night without your gloves." Aunt Louise turned off the television, went over, and held his wrist. "It's swelling. We need to get you to the emergency room."

Uncle Clem pulled his wrist away. "I think I'll see how that fire's doing." He started toward the living room but then stopped, looking down at his work boots.

"What is it?"

"My toes is numb." He started to walk again but almost lost his balance as he eased himself onto his cot. He looked at Aunt Louise. "Can't feel my feet."

Aunt Louise picked up the phone receiver. "Still dead." She put it down. "The Hudsons have gone to Connecticut. The Andersons spend Christmas with their in-laws. Who's left?" She turned to me, and I knew we were thinking the same thing.

I tore through the kitchen and down the back steps and through the icy, glittering garden. I opened the side gate that led to Mary Moore's field and jumped down into the frozen grass, which clicked against my pant legs as I ran. I stopped on the edge of the creek, knowing that I was acting against my uncle's wishes. There hadn't been a day since Mitchell died that Uncle Clem hadn't made some disparaging remark about Mr. Blakely. I think he did it out of a sense of guilt, believing that if he hadn't been friendly with Mr. Blakely in the first place, we wouldn't have been comfortable playing in the vicinity of that dog.

As I approached the house, the little dog, which remained tied up even in this weather, began yipping. A light flicked on the porch. Mr. Blakely's gray head appeared behind the screen. He stepped onto the porch, a napkin stuffed in his shirt. He was followed by his two grandsons. "Who's out there?" Mr. Blakely called, squinting into the dark. The way he said it reminded me that it hadn't been that long since he had received threats against his life.

"It's Jeru Lamb," I said. I started picking my way across the rocks but slipped and stepped into the freezing water, soaking my shoes. "My uncle has been bitten by a snake," I said, stepping onto the edge of Mr. Blakely's yard. "Our telephone isn't working."

"Ours neither," the old man said.

"Can you help us get him to the hospital?" I asked. One of the boys whispered something in his grandfather's ear. Mr. Blakely scratched his beard, studying me. The whole time, the dog barked and threw himself against the chain. "Behave, Tater." One of the boys raised his hand as if to smack it. The dog crept into its house.

"He is too heavy for me and my aunt to move," I pleaded.

Mr. Blakely told the boys to follow him inside. No one came back out. The dog growled from inside the doghouse. I remembered Uncle Clem yelling at Mr. Blakely the day Mitchell had been killed. I remembered his murderous tone and the way he had held the rifle. And how when he was working in the back of the garden, he would no longer acknowledge Mr. Blakely working his garden across the creek.

I started back to the house, wondering why I had ever believed Mr. Blakely might help and knowing Uncle Clem would be angry that I had asked.

"Hold up." Mr. Blakely came down off his porch, followed by his grandsons. They were dressed in coats and hats. "I don't have a car."

"He has that Model A," I said.

"That an antique, not a vehicle." Mr. Blakely took long strides so that the boys and I had to trot to keep up. We followed him across the creek and up through the garden. I pointed to the woodpile.

"It was that copperhead's widow," one of the boys said. "One he killed back in the fall and left in the creek to scare us."

Mr. Blakely paused at the bottom step. "Do he know we coming?"

"Not exactly."

Mr. Blakely stopped on the second step. "We wait out here while you go tell him."

"Please come on in." I was about to open the back door when Mr. Blakely spoke again.

"His gun?"

"It's down in his shop."

He motioned me to go on, and he followed. We found Aunt Louise sitting in the den across from Uncle Clem, who was looking very pale. Mr. Blakely and his boys waited at the edge of the den, their hats in their hands.

Uncle Clem sat up when he saw Mr. Blakely. He looked at me, then he looked at my aunt, as if we had betrayed him.

"Thank you for coming," Aunt Louise said.

"You can go home, Blakely." Uncle Clem tried to push himself up. "I don't need your help." He collapsed on his cot, touching his calf.

"Venom working its way up," Mr. Blakely said, noting a fact, rather than registering concern.

"I was bit in the arm." Uncle Clem held his wrist out, which was swollen to almost twice its normal size now.

"Don't matter where you bit." Mr. Blakely sniffed. "Death come from the ground up."

Uncle Clem looked at his feet, then at Mr. Blakely.

"Do you think we could carry him to the car?" Aunt Louise asked.

Mr. Blakely and I got on one side and the two boys got on the other, and we made a kind of seat and carried Uncle Clem to the front porch and set him in one of the rocking chairs.

Uncle Clem looked around. "I can't drive with these legs not working. Louise can't drive cause of her cataracts . . ."

Mr. Blakely disappeared down the driveway. In a minute there was a loud rumbling, then the sound of shots, the car backfiring. Mr. Blakely eased the Model A up the driveway, then we set Uncle Clem in the backseat. Aunt Louise climbed in with him. Mr. Blakely told his grandsons to go home and tell their grandmother he was driving Mr. Marshbanks to the hospital. I climbed into the passenger seat next to Mr. Blakely. He drove slowly since the streets were slick.

I had been surprised that Mr. Blakely was helping my uncle, but I shouldn't have been. In the sixties, in the South, if a white man asked a Negro for help of any kind, the Negro was expected to give it. And Mr. Blakely was even more beholden since his dog had killed my brother. By my simply asking him to help, I had given him no choice.

"It's up to my waist now, Blakely," Uncle Clem said from the backseat. "Like I'm sinking down."

Mr. Blakely looked at my uncle in the rearview mirror.

He drove deliberately, leaning forward with both hands on the wheel, and when he shifted the gears made a loud grinding noise. We passed Frank's Esso station with the lights on.

Uncle Clem rubbed away a circle of fog on the window glass with his jacket sleeve so he could see the neighborhood pass. "I sure wish I had a cigarette." Mr. Blakely reached inside his coat, took a pack of Camels out of his shirt pocket and handed it back to Clem. "Much obliged," said Clem, lighting a cigarette with a match, filling the car with thick smoke.

By the time we reached Greenville General, Uncle Clem was shivering. The attendants set him in a wheelchair and rolled him to the emergency room with us following behind. A nurse asked us to sit in the hallway. In a little while, a doctor came out and asked what kind of snake it was.

"It was too dark to see," I said, "maybe a copperhead," remembering Mr. Blakely's grandson's remark.

"That's likely." The doctor's beard was stubbled, as if he had been working a long shift. "We don't see many rattlesnake bites. He would probably be a lot sicker." He touched Aunt Louise's hand. "Your brother is going to be all right, Miss Marshbanks. Adults don't die from a copperhead bite. He might be sick for a few days." He walked back through the big swinging doors, which allowed us a glimpse of Uncle Clem, sitting on an examining table as a nurse rolled up his sleeve.

For the first time, I became aware of my wet pant legs and my soggy shoes. My feet were blocks of ice.

A nurse walked by and directed Mr. Blakely to sit in a

separate room for Negroes, but Aunt Louise said he was with us.

"It's all right." Mr. Blakely started to get up.

"Keep your seat." Aunt Louise stood, her voice shaking. "If you want to move him, you will have to move me first." Aunt Louise stepped between the nurse and the old man. The nurse, a strapping woman at least two heads taller than my aunt, could have easily lifted her with one hand and set her aside, but her face softened. "All right, ma'am."

The way Mr. Blakely held his hat in his hands and stared at the floor, I wasn't sure he wanted to stay, but then neither did he seem to want to contradict Aunt Louise. My aunt sat back down next to Mr. Blakely. She looked straight ahead, frowning to herself as if not quite certain what had come over her.

After a while she went off to find a phone to call my mother to tell her what had happened to Uncle Clem. I had wished she wouldn't call, since my father had probably missed his manuscript by now.

"I is sorry," Mr. Blakely said to me when we were alone.

"Don't you think he will be all right?" My teeth chattered from my cold clothes.

"I ain't talking about your uncle. He a tough old bird," he said. "I is talking about your brother."

"Oh." I looked at the floor, which was black-and-white squares like a giant chessboard. The old man had caught me off guard.

"That dog never bite nobody before. I had him since the day he born." He rubbed his palms, which were big and calloused. "If I had a-knowed he had that in him, I woulda drowned him when he a pup." He sighed. "Course I reckon people ain't much better. Don't none of us know what we *might* do till we does it." He looked at me with his black face and inscrutable yellow eyes.

"I 'preciate what your mama done," he said. "If she hadn't wrote that letter, we might've had to leave town." He sighed and stared off into space as if witnessing some unspeakable act. We sat for a while, not talking.

When my aunt returned from phoning my mother, I watched her face, looking for any hint of anger or confusion. I waited for her to tell me my father was on his way to pick me up. All she said was that my mother had asked if she should come to the hospital, and Aunt Louise had told her we had everything under control.

"Is that all she said?" I asked.

"That's all."

I shook my head. My father must have decided to keep his promise of not going down to his office until after Christmas. I had a reprieve until tomorrow morning.

I don't remember exactly how long we waited in the emergency room. I know it was hours. I remember Mr. Blakely bringing us coffee and doughnuts from the canteen. I was putting my socks and shoes back on, having dried them on a nearby radiator, when an orderly wheeled Uncle Clem out of the emergency room, followed by the doctor. Clem looked weak-eyed, but some of the color had already returned to his face. "Doc says I can go home."

The doctor patted my uncle on the shoulder. "Mr. Marshbanks has the constitution of an ox. His blood pressure is good and his pulse steady." He looked at Aunt Louise. "Keep a close eye on him for the next twenty-four hours."

The orderly allowed me to push the wheelchair, rolling my uncle down the hallway toward the door with Mr. Blakely and Louise following.

"Well, Blakely," said Uncle Clem over his shoulder, "for a minute there I thought I was a goner." He sounded very tired.

"We all goners, Mr. Marshbanks," said Mr. Blakely, "It's just the schedule that's in question." He tossed his coffee cup into a trash can and walked outside to the parking lot to get the car.

CHAPTER TEN

The Offspring of God

I ROLLED MY BIKE AROUND to the front yard but stopped when I heard the crackle of leaves coming from the magnolia tree. My heart pounded when I saw the silhouette of what looked like Mitchell perched on one of the lower limbs. He was wearing his big plaid coat and his old hat with earflaps that always made him look like a pilot. "Mitchell?" I called.

"Where are you going?" It was Henry's voice that came from the magnolia.

I stood there just looking at him. "For a ride," I said finally.

"Where?"

"I don't know." I watched my little brother climb higher up the tree. "Be careful," I said, pushing my bike up the drive.

I glanced across the street to see if Roger might be home. Somehow I was able to just look at his house and tell if he was there. He wasn't. He was often with his father on the weekends now.

It was a cold Saturday afternoon. I wore a heavy coat

with a hood and wool gloves. January had been unusually cold for Greenville. At night, the temperature dipped into the single digits, and during the day it never climbed above freezing. More sluggish parts of the Reedy had iced over. People didn't go anywhere unless they absolutely had to, and when they did, they warmed up their cars a good ten minutes beforehand.

Despite the weather, my mother had gone into work to write a story she wanted to finish before the baby came, which Dr. Norton predicted could be any day. My father had been typing in the basement. The miraculous had happened. He hadn't confronted me about his missing manuscript or mentioned it to my mother, although he clearly knew I was responsible. The day after Uncle Clem's snakebite, when I returned home, my father met me at the door. He didn't say a word, just looked into my face. I could feel that up until that moment he had struggled to reserve judgment. But then, as if the word "guilty" were printed across my forehead, he gave me a hurt look and turned away.

He didn't seem particularly angry. He didn't slam doors or throw the cat out of his lap. That would have been easier for me to watch. Instead, he seemed profoundly disappointed. After a few days, I understood that he wasn't going to confront me. Having raised us to own up to our mistakes, he wanted me to come to him. And when I didn't, I think he saw it as much his own failure as mine.

I believe my mother attributed his behavior to the fact that it had finally hit him that he was having to return to work and that he was running out of time to finish his book. And in a way, she was right. The remarkable thing is how, from the day after Christmas, he went down to his office and resumed typing. And he had continued going down there, day after day. The only difference I detected was that he typed even faster. Once, when he had gone out for cigarettes, I had sneaked down to his office but found it locked. He had never locked it before. I went outside and peered through the basement window. I was shaken to see a small, neat stack of manuscript pages where the other one had been. He had started over, from scratch, without a word to anyone. The sight of that stack pained me, and from then on, whenever I heard him type, each key tapped my conscience.

I rode past the mansions on Crescent Avenue, which in this cold weather seemed even more imposing and severe. The street made me lonely. I wished Roger could have come with me. He had a way of absolving me of my guilt by making light of it, which, if an adult had done it, would have been belittling. But Roger dismissed my worries in a way that acknowledged them at the same time.

I turned off Crescent Avenue and started down Jones, a street more like my own. I turned onto Tindall and stopped in front of Donaldson. On the playground, the drinking fountain had frozen into an uneven row of stalactites. I got off my bike and sat in a swing, the cold chains hurting my gloved hands.

The school windows were dark. I no longer dreaded school. I looked forward to Mrs. Watts reading to us from *Charlotte's Web* or teaching us to play "The Erie Canal" on the tonette or showing us how to construct a hygrometer out of a milk carton and a strand of our own hair. She even played kickball with us on the playground. But sometimes, in the middle of one of these activities, I missed the suspense of Miss Hawkins. In a way it felt that as formidable as she could sometimes be, she had taken us more seriously. Because she had moved to North Carolina, we never even saw her around town anymore. Sometimes Roger and I rode past her house in case she had returned, but the lights were never on. She had walked out of our classroom and into oblivion.

From the swing, I could make out a few of the Negro houses through the leafless trees. Sweet wood smoke hung in the air—a dark, almost purplish gauze that enwrapped the neighborhood. Window lights eyed me through the trees. I wondered what I was doing at my school on a Saturday afternoon. I did not know I had visited the school as a kind of transition—a jumping-off place.

A week before, I had come close to telling my father what I had done but had told him something else instead. I had been unable to sleep and tiptoed down to the basement and stood outside my father's office door. I knocked. He didn't answer. I knocked again. The typing stopped. I didn't move, didn't breathe. He opened the door. "What is it?" He put his hand behind my head, leading me into his office, which was one big cloud of smoke. The red-coiled space heater whirred in the corner.

"I don't feel good."

"What hurts?" he asked, starting to unlock his medicine drawer.

I looked at the bare walls where all his sketches had been. I noted the new stack of manuscript on his desk, which had grown since I had peeked through his office window. It was now about a third of what the original had been. The sight of that stack made me proud of my father and terribly ashamed of myself.

"What hurts, Jeru?"

I placed my hand on my stomach.

"Too many of Della's black-eyed peas," he said, unlocking his desk drawer and extracting a pink bottle of Pepto-Bismol and the sticky spoon. "I have never understood how Southerners can eat black-eyed peas. Have the texture of sawdust." He spooned the thick pink liquid into my mouth, which I imagined coating my stomach like the glass globe in the TV commercial. "That should settle things," he said, putting the bottle and the spoon in his desk and locking it.

I picked up the snow-scene paperweight and shook it. The snow reminded me of ashes.

"Was there anything else?" My father glanced at his typewriter, reading over what he had written.

I paused there in my flannel button-up pajamas, unable to move from the spot, as if my body, upon demanding something of me, had seized up. "Norma Jones is your daughter," I said.

My father looked up. "What was that?"

"Norma, the girl we took to Dr. Norton's, the girl who sits next to me in class. She is your daughter."

My father stood up, walked around his desk, and faced me. "How do you know this?"

"She told me. Her mother had said I was Norma's half brother and that you were Norma's father. Norma said they moved here from Wilmington after her stepfather died of cancer and her mother was transferred to her new job at Belk's."

My father stared at me until he didn't see me anymore. He walked over to the window and looked out at the black night, his hands in his pockets. He stood there forever. I couldn't see his face.

"Norma," he said to himself, "Norma Jones." Until that moment, he had not even known his daughter's name. Finally, he looked at me. "What is she like?" His voice was quiet.

"She's the best speller in the class. She does all the math problems faster than anyone. They say she has the highest IQ in the whole county." I could see by his faraway look that I was not telling him what he needed to know.

"All this time," he said to himself as he looked out the window.

I ran my finger along the edge of his desk. "What are you going to do?" I asked.

"Do?" he said, still looking out the window.

"Are you going to leave us and go live with them?"

He turned to me. A more thoughtless father might have laughed at such a ridiculous question, but my father, who never condescended to us, just smiled sadly. This was enough to tell me he wasn't doing anything of the kind.

He came over to me, putting his hand on my shoulder. "We all make choices, Jeru. Choices we have to live with." He paused. "Or live without." He shook his head. "She has her family." He looked at me. "And I have mine."

"What about the letters? Why were you looking for her?"

"I needed to know where she was." He sat at his desk. He unlocked his desk drawer, pulled out a Bayer bottle, and took three aspirin, washing them down with swallows of cold coffee. He looked at me. "Does your mother know about this?"

"I haven't told her."

"Let's keep it between us, at least until after the baby has come." He closed the medicine drawer, locking it.

"Yes, sir." I nodded.

He looked up at me. "You know what I have learned, Jeru?"

"No, sir."

"To regard all dharmas as dreams." His voice cracked when he said this.

I stood there, like I had so many times before, with no idea what he had just said, yet having the distinct impression that something beyond his words and their meaning had gotten through to me. But I did not know how to show him this.

He stared at the sheet in his typewriter. I felt bad about leaving him. I wanted to tell him what I came down to tell him. Instead, I went back to bed and didn't hear him type any more that night.

I RODE TOWARD AUGUSTA ROAD, then turned down Mill's Avenue, crossing into the spare neighborhood of white clapboard houses that led to the brick mill—its water tower rising over the neighborhood like a giant thimble. I had driven past the mill with my parents almost every day of my life, but I had never stood in its shadow. The mill houses were closer together than the houses of my neighborhood but were not as cramped as Della's. Front yards were small squares of well-maintained grass parted by concrete walks. Cramped backyards consisted of a clothesline, a small vegetable patch, and perhaps a car in mid-repair.

I caught sight of Norma's house down the street and

stopped one house away. Her mother's Volkswagen was in the driveway. There were lights in the kitchen window, and I saw someone, maybe Norma, at the table, with her head bent as if reading.

I leaned my bike against a tree and watched the house. Norma and I had spoken a little more since school had started again in January. I had thanked her for *John F. Kennedy and PT-109,* and we consulted about math problems or grammar questions. We were more comfortable around each other than we had been before Christmas. We had begun to accept each other on more intimate terms but conversationally were at a loss as to how to proceed.

I knocked. A short, slightly plump woman with wire-rimmed glasses, her hair pulled back in a bun, opened the door. "Can I help you?" she asked. She wore a blue cardigan, which she had buttoned all the way to her neck. She had on a plain skirt and a pair of flat-heeled shoes. She looked more like a librarian than a clothes buyer. Adding to the effect, she held a book in her hand, her finger marking her place.

"Is Norma here?" I asked, my teeth chattering, a combination of cold and fear.

"Who is it, Mama?" Norma called. I could see her in the kitchen, where she sat doing homework. Even if I hadn't seen her, I would have known I was at the right place. I smelled toast.

"Someone to see you," her mother said. "Come in before you catch your death." She pulled me in rather brusquely and closed the door.

Norma ran in from the kitchen. "Your mother had the baby?"

"Not yet," I said, feeling self-conscious with her mother standing there. "Dr. Norton said it could be any time."

Norma looked at her mother, who was watching me now as if she had realized who she had let into her house. "Mama, this is Jeru Lamb."

"I have met your mother at PTA meetings," Mrs. Jones said in a reserved tone. I was surprised to discover that the two women had actually met. I couldn't help wondering what would have happened if it hadn't been for my father's aversion to meetings.

Norma showed me a hook behind the door, where I hung my coat, then led me to the gas stove in the middle of the living room. I warmed myself, looking around. Like our house, the walls were lined with bookshelves, but these were made of cinder blocks and boards, and instead of neat hardbacks all in a row, these were crowded with paperbacks, broken-backed and fattened from having been read. They were stuffed into the shelves, stacked on one another, wedged in anyway they would fit. Potted plants grew on top of the bookshelves, long vines hooking down over the books.

Norma led me to the kitchen while her mother, without saying another word, sat down at one end of the stuffed couch and started reading. Norma's social-studies book and her notebook were open on the Formica table. The smell of toast was strongest here.

"Don't mind her," Norma whispered, nodding toward her mother. She told me to sit in a chair at the kitchen table, as she began to mix milk and Nestlé Quik into a saucepan over a gas ring that reminded me of Aunt Louise's stove.

Norma lowered the flame on the saucepan, then sat in the chair across from me. She shoved her books to the side. "All right," she said. "What is it?"

I looked out the window that I had just been looking in. I felt a little crack in the wall that had been building in me over the past weeks. "I did something," I said, glancing in the direction of the living room. From where we sat, Norma's mother was around the corner, out of sight.

Norma got up and turned on the little radio on the counter. It was tuned to the easy-listening station. The station my mother also liked. The station they kept on at the doctor's office. To me, the music all sounded the same, a single endless melancholy song.

"She can't hear us now," Norma said, sitting back down.

I felt the wall crack a little more. "I burned up my father's book."

"You did?" She scooted her chair a little closer to the table. "How come?"

I shrugged. "One minute I was looking at all those pages and the next minute they were in the middle of the fire."

She pushed a strand of hair back out of her face. "Kind of like you were a robot?"

"Kind of."

She leaned toward me. "That happens to me."

"It does?" I found myself leaning toward her. I had never realized how green her eyes were, like the green of new leaves.

"Sometimes when I'm real mad or real sad or real *anything*," she said. "It's like somebody else is at the controls."

We looked at each other a minute, our faces only inches apart. Then, inexplicably, she kissed my cheek. I sat back, my face gone hot. Norma sat back, not looking the least flustered. "Like that," she said matter-of-factly. "I didn't know I was going to do that."

Embarrassed though I was, I could still feel where her lips had brushed my cheek, and how in that second all the things that were whirling around in my head had stopped, and every terrible mistake I had made and every terrible mistake I was going to make were lifted from me, and for the briefest of moments, my world was still.

There was a sizzling sound on the stove. The hot chocolate boiled over, running down the outside of the pot. Norma jumped up to cut off the flame.

"Everything all right in there?" Norma's mother called from the living room.

"Yes, ma'am." Norma poured the hot chocolate, handing me a cup. Then she set a plate of saltines on the table and sat back down. She dipped a saltine in her hot chocolate and popped it in her mouth. "Go ahead," she said. "It's good."

Still a little dazed, I dipped a saltine in the hot chocolate, but mine disintegrated, leaving white globs floating on the surface.

"You left it in too long," she said and, picking up another saltine, demonstrated how to dip it quickly. I tried again and this time the saltine held together long enough to make it to my mouth. We drank our hot chocolate and dipped our saltines in silence. Occasionally, the wind rattled the windows.

"When my daddy died," Norma finally said, her voice soft, "I didn't think I would ever get over it." She tipped up her empty cup for the last of the chocolate. "And you don't get over it." She set her cup down, wiping her mouth with the back of her hand. "You just stop expecting them to walk in the room."

I drank my hot chocolate, wondering why she had said that. Was she trying to tell me she knew how I was feeling about Mitchell? Or was she simply telling me something that mattered most to her? I picked up Norma's social-studies book, then set it back down.

"Daddy knows about you," I heard myself say. "I told him."

"That's OK," Norma said, as if she had expected me to tell him. I couldn't help wondering if by her telling me that I shouldn't tell my father, she had somehow made it easier for me to tell him.

We sat in the kitchen a little longer. Since I had finished my hot chocolate, I ate the rest of the saltines. She got up and washed our cups and put them in the drain. I remember thinking that was something Della would do, but, then, Norma didn't have a Della.

Norma walked me to the front door, lifting down my coat.

"Wait a minute," Norma's mother said, getting up from the couch. She went over to one of the bookshelves and pulled down a gilt-edged book, wiping the dust with her sweater sleeve. She glanced at Norma, then thrust the book at me. "I have meant to return this to your father for years," she said.

"Yes, ma'am," I said, tucking the book in my coat.

Norma's mother turned away abruptly and went into the kitchen.

"She doesn't know what to do with you," Norma whispered. "Sometimes I'm not real sure either." Then she pressed my hand. "Tell me when the baby comes."

It wasn't until I had said good-bye and was standing out on the sidewalk that I pulled the book out and saw it was a hardback of *Walden.* When I read the title, I thought of the little cabin up in the mountains we had passed on our drives. The pond would be frozen thick.

On the flyleaf, inscribed in ornate cursive, was the name Thomas Franklin Lamb—my great-grandfather. So my father had at least partially told the truth. He really had tried to track down this book.

I thought about Norma telling me how difficult it had been when her stepfather died, and the way she had said it made it clear that even though my father was her biological father, this man who had died of cancer had been her true father. I was ashamed for never having considered what a blow that must have been.

I looked back at Norma's house, saw Norma in the kitchen window, her head bent to her books, and remembered her kiss. Norma's mother appeared in the window, standing over her daughter and looking in my direction.

UNCLE CLEM HAD PARKED HIMSELF in the front room, watching football. My mother and I were with Aunt Louise in her bedroom, helping pack. We had left my father typing and Henry rearranging his collections. For the past three Sunday afternoons, my mother and I had helped Aunt Louise pack.

Aunt Louise had begged my mother not to do any more because Dr. Norton said she should rest. My mother couldn't abide rest. She promised Aunt Louise she wouldn't lift anything. I helped move boxes as soon as the adults had them packed, and I carried empty boxes up from the basement. My mother taped boxes while Aunt Louise wrote labels. Since Clem and Louise were only allowed a few personal items at the nursing home, everything else was to be divided between Uncle Charlie's family and ours.

Uncle Clem hadn't protested any more about moving into the nursing home, but he wasn't helping either. The burden of packing and leaving the house in order had fallen to Aunt Louise. Part of Uncle Clem's ambivalence might have been due to the snakebite. He had seemed listless ever since. Although Dr. Norton found nothing physically wrong, he said a scare like that could affect someone psychologically. He predicted Clem would snap out of it in a few weeks.

My mother had opened a cedar chest at the foot of Aunt Louise's bed and started folding and packing quilts. I hadn't seen my mother with this much energy since before she was pregnant. It was as if she wanted to get the whole world straight before the baby came or, and I couldn't help thinking this, before she wasn't around to straighten it.

My aunt had said for what must have been the sixth time that my mother must not overdo it when she noticed my mother staring at the floor. "What is it, honey?" my aunt said.

A little puddle had appeared beneath my mother, as if she had peed in the middle of Aunt Louise's bedroom.

"I think my water broke." My mother stood up, feeling the back of her skirt. When she turned around, we could see a dark wet spot.

"Should we call the doctor?" asked Aunt Louise, getting up.

"All it means is that the baby will be here within forty-eight hours," my mother said. "That's how it has been with the others." She hurried off to the bathroom while Aunt Louise went through her closet, looking for something my mother could change into.

Feeling this was suddenly woman's territory, I wandered down the hall to find Uncle Clem. He wasn't sitting on his cot. He wasn't in the kitchen either. But the back door was cracked open, letting in cold air. I looked out. He was sitting on the bottom step in his jacket and cap, smoking a cigarette. I grabbed my coat off the kitchen table and walked down the steps.

"What're you doing out here?" I asked, sitting down beside him.

Clem stared out at the garden, which was mostly a field of dirt now and a few brown stalks.

"Mama's water just broke," I said, blowing into my hands. I had no clear idea what it meant, but since it seemed to generate such excitement I thought he ought to know.

He took a drag on his cigarette and squinted out at the garden. I sat there a long time with him. I could hear the pigeons on the roof. Now and then they would peek down at us as if keeping an eye on Uncle Clem. A couple even dared to fly down in front of us, strutting in the grass. Clem hadn't so much as picked up his gun since he had come back from the hospital. And as far as I knew he hadn't set foot in his workshop.

Clem took another drag on his cigarette. "I had a dream last night."

"Yes, sir?" I crossed my arms, trying to stay warm.

"Dreamed I died."

I looked at him.

"And went to Heaven," he said, tapping his ashes on the steps. "And that I met the Man Hisself."

"You dreamed you met Jesus?" I searched my uncle's face for a hint of a smile, but I had never seen him more serious.

Uncle Clem glanced back toward the house, then lowered his voice. "Shook my hand. Firm grip. Reckon He could have rolled that boulder back Hisself on Easter morning. Even let me finger His thorny crown." He looked back at the house again. "I don't want Louise getting wind of this. She might try to make me into a prayer warrior." He took one last puff of his cigarette, then ground it into the concrete at the bottom of the stairs. "And I'll tell you one more thing if you can keep a secret."

"Yes, sir," I whispered.

He leaned over. He looked very frail. "Jesus is a colored. Skin black as soot." He studied the garden and then the Negro houses beyond. "Which ain't the best of news for my heavenly prospects."

We sat there a while longer. By now, several pigeons had flown down and paced in front of us. I pictured a Negro Jesus trying to sit down to the Last Supper and the white disciples not letting Him in.

"Let's go back inside. This is unnatural cold." Clem pulled himself to his feet and started up the stairs. He stopped and looked down at me. "You coming?"

I shook my head and looked out at the garden.

"I could make us some coffee."

"No, thanks," I said, not turning around.

"Suit yourself." He went inside.

I hopped up and ran toward the garden, having had enough of Clem. I stopped by the frozen goldfish pond and watched for orange flashes beneath the ice. Why did adults think they were the only ones with problems?

A little dust-colored bird flew up out of the garden. Roger would have known the kind. Somehow the bird reminded me of Norma, and the knot in my stomach untwisted a little. I walked through the garden, thinking about my visit with her and how I could still faintly feel the brush of her lips on my cheek. It embarrassed me to think about it, but behind the embarrassment was comfort. I hadn't given my father *Walden* yet. It hadn't felt like the right time.

I passed by the toolshed and the old henhouse and paused at the gate to the Moores' field. Finally, I opened the gate and stepped down into the tall grass, not hearing a peep out of Mr. Blakely's dog. I stood there remembering Mitchell, thinking this might be one of the last times I would ever visit this place. I lay down in the tall grass and hid. My fingers pressed against the cold ground. I shut my eyes and listened to the grass rustle whenever the wind blew. Over on Augusta Road, beyond the Negro houses, a train rumbled.

Someone called me. I didn't jump up at first but lay there, with my eyes closed, smelling grass and earth. I gradually raised my head, keeping low. My father was on the balcony, his hands to his mouth as he called across the garden. "Jeeee-ruuuu!" My mother must have phoned him. Maybe things were happening faster than she had thought. I ran fast through the field, remembering us try-

ing to get away from the dog and how the grass had
slowed us.

DELLA SPENT THE NIGHT with Henry and me, since my
father had taken my mother to the hospital. She fed us a
supper of cold meat loaf, applesauce, and a slice of white
bread (to which I added ketchup and Duke's mayonnaise).
She let us watch Ed Sullivan.

My father had called twice from the hospital, but all
Henry and I heard was Della saying, "All right, then,
Mr. Lamb. All right, then." The first time she got off the
phone saying the baby hadn't come yet and that Mama
said for us to be good. The second time she said they were
going to operate and that Daddy said we didn't have to go
to school tomorrow. I could tell by the way Della kept
telling us everything was going to be all right how worried
she was.

Della had spent the night whenever my mother and my
father went for a long weekend in the mountains, which
they did every couple of years. She didn't sleep in our parents' bedroom but made her bed on the couch in the den.
She stayed up late with the TV on, reading one of her
shiny-covered romances and smoking.

After she tucked us in bed, I waited until I heard her
settle in the den before I turned on my flashlight, climbed
out of bed, and tiptoed into my parents' bedroom. I
flipped through the phone book until I found Norma's
phone number. When Norma's mother answered, I told
her who I was. There was a pause as if she were making
up her mind, then she said, "Just a minute."

"The baby?" Norma asked when she came to the phone.

"They are operating tonight," I said.

"Why are you whispering?"

"Della doesn't know I'm on the phone."

"Don't be worried," Norma said.

"I better go."

"Everything will be fine."

"I have to go," I said and hung up.

I noticed my mother's copy of *Science and Health* by the phone. The book fell open to a paragraph she had underlined. I shined my flashlight on the page:

"The offspring of God start not from matter or ephemeral dust. They are in and of Spirit, Divine Mind, and so forever continue."

From what I could decode, Mary Baker Eddy was talking about the dead, but Mitchell hadn't continued forever, unless she meant the way the rest of us continued missing him. I kept flipping through the book, reading my mother's underlined passages. Reading Mary Baker Eddy left me with the same unsettled feeling I had whenever I attended Sunday school. From what I could gather, my spiritual side wandered murky, treacherous terrain somewhere between comprehension and faith.

I tiptoed into Henry's room, where he was already asleep, his fingers in his mouth and his knees on the floor as if he were praying. I swung his legs into bed, surprised at how heavy he had gotten. I lay down beside him, listening to him breathe, watching his eyelids pulse. His hair smelled dusty and sweet.

Sometime much later, when I was in a deep sleep, I dreamed of speaking to Thomas Edison. He was telling me what a fine woman my aunt was and how he would have given up the lightbulb for her. "But she turned me down," he said with a sigh, "said she needed to care for your family, said all your mothers quit early." In the middle of my dream, a phone began to ring. Edison cocked his head at the ringing and said, "I didn't invent that."

CHAPTER ELEVEN

Spy Plane

MY MOTHER LAY TOO STILL. Her eyes were closed, and her arms hung lifelessly by her sides. The sleeve of her hospital gown didn't quite hide the plastic name tag clipped around her wrist. They had banded her like a bird. Someone had pulled her hair back in a strange way, making her face seem frail and gaunt. Her neck was pale as paper. The afternoon light fell across the room, making long shadows.

This was what it was like when a patient died on one of Della's soap operas, except the dying person usually started to say something, but then their eyes fluttered, their head lolled back, and they never finished their sentence. But that was on television. I had seen the real thing up close.

I turned to my father, puzzled and angry that he hadn't prepared me on the way over. He hadn't even seemed upset. What kind of man was he? He had explained that Dr. Norton had been on the verge of operating when the baby came almost by itself. After the baby was delivered, Dr. Norton wanted to keep my mother in the hospital a few days for observation. That was all my father had said. He certainly hadn't mentioned anybody dying.

I had been so absorbed in my mother that I hadn't noticed Aunt Louise in the vinyl chair by the window, a blanket in her arms. "Come on over here, Jeru," she said, pulling the blanket back, revealing a wrinkled red thing with a mouth.

I stepped back.

Aunt Louise held the blanket out to me.

I slipped behind my father, putting him between me and the baby.

"She's beautiful." Aunt Louise handed the baby to my father.

My father cradled the baby in his arms, while she gurgled and flexed her scrawny fingers. "Jeru, say hello to Ruth," my father said.

I peered over the blanket. I had been too young to visit the hospital when Mitchell and Henry were born, and my mother hadn't come home with either of them for a couple of weeks. By the time they did come home, they had filled out, looking more like Gerber babies than like this alien-skinned thing my father held against his chest.

I touched her open hand, and, like a tiny trap, her fingers sprang closed over mine, squeezing tightly as if she recognized me.

My mother sat up in bed, yawning and stretching. She held out her arms to me, but I did not move, could not move. It was as if the momentum of months anticipating the worst, months rehearsing an unfathomable grief, had come to a simple and sudden end. My body could not keep pace with my emotions, and I stood paralyzed in the middle of the room.

"Jeru?" My mother's voice was something I had never expected to hear again.

I threw myself into her arms, nearly knocking her over. I hugged her, feeling the substantialness of her, feeling how much I required her. And as she held me, it was more than relief that I felt; it was salvation but not of a spiritual kind. It was a salvation of the senses. At the same time, I felt a remote tinge of disappointment, as if my mother's living had derailed the tragic story I had been telling myself.

"What is this?" She tapped the book I had forgotten I carried under my arm. I handed her her copy of *Science and Health.* I had thought she might want it.

My mother frowned as if she weren't particularly happy to see it, but then she began flipping through the pages. She turned to a page with a sentence underlined in pen. "Here it is," she said to herself and read aloud, " 'Multiplication of God's children comes from no power of propagation in matter, it is the reflection of Spirit.' "

"Are you saying we had nothing to do with her?" My father nodded to the baby in his arms.

"That is what Mary Baker Eddy is saying." My mother closed the book and set it on her night table. It was the first time I remember my mother's distinguishing between Mary Baker Eddy's beliefs and her own.

"Henry wanted me to give you this." I took an empty snail shell out of my pocket. Henry had to stay home with Della since the hospital didn't allow children under seven on the halls.

My mother held the snail shell in her palm.

My father stroked the baby's head. He glanced up at Aunt Louise. "Did Charlie bring you over?"

She nodded. "Clem said he didn't want to get near the hospital again any time soon. He said he will see Ruth at home."

The baby started to whimper. My father jiggled her in his arms, but the baby cried more, its hands jerked open and closed. I stroked her head, feeling grateful to her for not taking my mother.

I don't remember precisely when Norma appeared in the doorway holding a bouquet of jonquils. It took me a minute to recognize her. She wore a new velvet dress that seemed a size too big and new patent-leather shoes. Her hair was combed and tied with a bow. I had never thought of Norma as pretty before. She was catching her breath as if she had been running, and she kept looking back down the hall. She stepped inside as a nurse hurried past the door.

"Norma." My father hesitated, then he took a couple of steps toward her. Norma didn't say anything, but the look that passed between them was a silent acknowledgment. She looked at the baby cradled in his arms, staring at it for a long time.

"Muriel," my father said, clearing his throat, "this is Norma Jones." He paused, as if making a decision. "The little girl Jeru and I drove to Dr. Norton's office."

"Please come in." My mother sat up in her bed. "I remember your mother from the PTA."

Norma handed her the jonquils. She turned around, keeping the baby in sight.

"Is your mother outside?" my father asked, still holding the baby. He stepped into the hallway, perhaps thinking he might cut her off. My heart pounded.

"I came by myself," Norma said, her voice cracking a little.

"I didn't think they allowed children up here without an adult." My mother smelled the flowers. "Where did you get jonquils in the middle of the winter?" I could tell by the way she didn't take her eyes off Norma that she was more than a little puzzled why the girl had come.

Aunt Louise held out her hand to Norma.

"This is Louise," my father said, coming back beside Norma. "Jeru's great-aunt."

I didn't know what Norma might do or say. But now, as I watched her watching the baby, it made sense that she had come. Of course she wanted to see the baby.

"Pleased to meet you," said Aunt Louise.

The baby began to cry, and my mother set the jonquils on the night table and picked up a full baby bottle. "You ready for lunch, Ruth?" she asked as my father laid the baby in her arms.

"A sister." Norma put her hand on my shoulder. "What do you think about that?" Her voice had an edge to it that made me tug at my shirt collar. Her eyes reddened as she watched my mother work the nipple into the baby's mouth. "She's hungry." Norma leaned over so far to see the baby she was practically in my mother's lap.

"Do you like babies?" my mother asked.

Norma stroked its arm. "I like this baby."

My mother looked up at my father.

Norma placed her finger in the baby's hand. "Y'all must be very happy." She turned around to my father.

"Yes," he said to her in a quiet tone. "But she doesn't replace what has been lost." He gave her shoulder a squeeze, pulled her against him, and then let go. My mother had been watching but seemed to dismiss my father's behavior as due to one of his passionate mystical moments.

A tear streaked Norma's cheek as she looked back at the baby. I stepped up beside Norma and held out my Kit Carson handkerchief, which, to my relief, she accepted.

THE NEXT MORNING WAS SATURDAY. Roger and I had gotten up early and ridden our bikes to the Reedy. On my way out, I had poured Henry a bowl of Alpha-Bits. I left him eating cereal and studying various medicine bottles of insects he had lined up in front of his bowl. My father was still asleep. He had typed most of the night, hoping to take advantage of these last days before my mother returned with the baby.

Since it was clear that my mother was alive and that this arrangement of my father, Henry, and me was not permanent, I suddenly felt on holiday from being mothered. My father didn't inspect our hands before meals, didn't insist we eat our vegetables (in fact, seldom cooked vegetables), and didn't stand over us while we brushed our teeth. He didn't have us pick up our dirty clothes or take out the trash. That weekend, the three of us reveled in a male squalor which was that much sweeter because we knew that we would probably never be alone together again. After all, not just one female was returning from the hospital.

It was an unusually mild morning for February. Winter had backed off in the past couple of days. Roger and I pushed our bikes beside the river, along a soft path smelling of crushed pine needles. I was feeling better than I had since that morning back in September when my mother first intimated she might be pregnant. To me, the months that followed had been nothing less than a count-down to her demise. I had not considered the baby as any-thing more than a means to my mother's end. Now, not only did I have my mother back, but I was getting a sister in the bargain.

I was happy to be outside, in Roger's company. I knew full well I had other worries, but they seemed, momentar-ily at least, small. The morning was bright. Some birds Roger identified as Carolina wrens were actually singing. Even the Reedy appeared a little less clouded. Roger, too, seemed, if not happy, then less brooding. His mood had gradually improved over the past month as he had ad-justed to the idea of his parents living separately. "At least they aren't fighting," he had said more than once.

We pushed our bikes onto the meadow with the jet plane mounted in the middle. We laid our bikes in the grass and stood in the shadow of a wing, gripping the wrought-iron fence that kept children like us from climb-ing all over the plane. We stared up at the empty cockpit.

"I wonder if the pilot had a family?" Roger asked.

It was a startling question—one that I wouldn't have been equipped to ponder earlier and one Roger probably wouldn't have thought to ask. But now that our immediate world was a little less ominous, we could afford to see slightly beyond ourselves.

We spent the rest of the morning down by the Reedy, skipping rocks, scrambling over its grassy banks, then ending up on an arched stone footbridge, dangling our legs over a creek that joined the Reedy. We had taken out our pocketknives and were shaving the bark off sticks. Roger's father had given him a new pocketknife. He gave Roger a present whenever he picked him up.

We had been whittling for some time when Roger caught me looking at him.

"What?" he asked.

"I was just thinking . . ."

"Uh-oh," Roger said, carefully curling off a piece of bark and letting it drop into the creek below. "What now?"

"I don't feel all that bad anymore," I said, returning to my whittling.

Now Roger was looking at me. "And isn't that good?"

"I guess." I shaved off the last of the bark and felt the clean, smooth wood. "I'm just not used to it."

Roger looked out across the river. "I know what you mean."

When we finished our sticks, we dropped them into the clear creek and watched them drift out into the river, where they gained momentum and eventually floated out of sight.

B. Y.'S BARBERSHOP WAS NOT CROWDED. My father, his hair neatly parted and glistening with hair tonic, flipped through a *Life* magazine, waiting for Henry and me. He was a handsome man, and sitting there, in his coat and tie, a cigarette in the corner of his mouth, he looked like an ad for Lucky Strikes. Getting our hair cut was the one thing he had required of us that weekend. He wanted us presentable for our mother's homecoming. A haircut was also part of his preparation for starting back at the agency. As soon as the baby had arrived, he was more willing, even a little eager, to return to his old job.

Henry was in the chair next to mine, getting his hair cut by B. Y., a short, soft-spoken man. From his chair at the front of the barbershop, B. Y. presided over three other barbers. I sat next to Henry, getting my hair cut by Leon—a bald string bean of a man who had been cutting hair for as long as B. Y. had.

Leon had finished cutting my hair and was scraping off the warm lather behind my ears with a straight razor. I could see Henry in the mirror. He had to sit on a board placed across the chair. B. Y. had started on him, passing the electric razor through my brother's curls. In the mirror, he resembled Mitchell so much that I looked to actually make sure he wasn't him.

"Careful, son," Leon said, lifting the razor. "You'll be wanting that ear."

I straightened, staring into the mirror in front of me, which reflected the mirror behind me, which reflected back to the mirror in front; smaller and smaller reflections of me sank deep into the wall.

I heard Henry ask B. Y., "If the world is round, why can't we see the curves?"

"I have often wondered that myself," said B. Y., combing my brother's hair.

When Leon finished shaving the back of my neck, he wiped away the rest of the lather with a warm towel. He unclipped the bib around my neck and shook it. He opened the drawer behind his chair. I chose an orange sucker, then stepped off the chair and sat beside my father. We both watched B. Y. cut Henry's hair.

I relished coming here with my father. This was before the time of "hairstyling," which not only inflated prices but put an end to barbershops as safe havens for boys and their fathers. At B. Y.'s, few girls came in, and then it was usually with their fathers. The men joked in a way that made me feel a part of them, even if I didn't understand the jokes. I liked the sharp smell of hair tonic, the worn softness of the leather chairs, and the sound of the electric razors droning like a squadron of B-52s.

I was thinking about what I still had not told my father. I did not feel as bad about burning his manuscript as I had. My mother's living had altered everything, letting light in everywhere. I felt capable of confessing. So the whole way over to B. Y.'s I had sat in the backseat, trying to decide when to tell him. Now, with the electric razors going, seemed like the best time to not be overheard by anyone else. I must have also considered that he couldn't kill me in public.

I tugged on my father's sleeve.

"Uh-huh?" He put down his magazine.

I leaned over and said in a low voice, "I burned your book."

His smile faded. Somebody had told a joke down at the other end of the barbershop and everybody was laughing. He looked at me. He looked out the window at all the cars parked there. His jaw was working, a sure sign that he was agitated. Then he looked back at me. "Well, I must say, Jeru, it is about time."

"You knew?"

I saw that Henry was watching us now, and even though he couldn't hear over the noise of B. Y.'s electric razor, I could tell by the look on his face that he knew I had confessed.

"I have wondered why, though." My father put away the magazine. "Was it because you found out about having a sister? Were you getting back at me?"

"I didn't plan it," I said.

My father sat back in his chair, lit another cigarette, and

watched B. Y. cut Henry's hair. Now and then, he looked at me, as if he was deciding what should be done with me. It wasn't until B. Y. had finished and was lifting Henry down from the board that my father threw down his cigarette and crushed it on the worn tile. He took a deep breath and said, "It was fate."

"What?"

"You were an instrument of fate."

"What do you mean?"

"This revision is already much stronger, and I wouldn't have written it if you hadn't burned the first draft." He stood and pulled out his wallet to pay B. Y. as Henry was reaching into B. Y.'s drawer for a sucker. I sat in my seat, astonished and more than a little distrustful of my father's reaction.

I licked my orange sucker and thought how adults were never as angry or hurt or upset as I expected, as if they had something else in them to fall back on. The only real sign of anger came when he handed down our coats from the rack by the front door. He leaned over and said to me, "Don't let it happen again," and then zipped up my coat roughly. "This is my last revision."

When we were getting into the car, Henry climbed into the backseat with me. He seemed pleased. It was against his nature to keep anything from anybody, and it had taken all his concentration not to tell on me.

"Who am I, the chauffeur?" asked my father, patting the empty passenger seat beside him. He sounded irritated. He started the car and pulled out of the parking lot and onto Augusta Road. He turned on the radio. Henry crouched on his knees and drew a cat with his finger in the fog of the back window.

We passed the Lewis Plaza, the post office, and Frank's Esso. I felt better than I had felt in a long time. My mother was alive and well, the baby healthy, and my father less than furious about what I had done.

"Why did God make some of our fingers longer?" Henry held his hand out to me as if it were something he had just found.

I pressed my hand against his and felt a warmth travel down my arm and across my chest—like an electric shock except softer. A palpable, if tenuous, happiness.

CHAPTER TWELVE

The Man Upstairs

ROGER AND I PAUSED AT THE TOP of Donaldson's steps, shook Mr. Keener's hand, and blinked into the sun. We had to hold ourselves back as we walked down the steps. On the sidewalk, we flung our notebooks into the clear June sky and watched a year's worth of graded papers settle across the trampled grass. We trotted up the sidewalk, away from spelling bees and long division, away from overhead projectors and chalk dust, away from corn dogs and congealed fruit salad.

We cheered as Ricky McIntire bashed his flour-paste map of Spain against the school fence, as Billy Bukowski sat on his clay model of Vesuvius, as Gwyn Youngblood cut her math exercise book into paper dolls, as Millicent Dillingham did a vicious little dance on her poster of the life cycle of a luna moth.

Roger and I said longer good-byes to some of the Mill's Mill children, knowing we wouldn't see them until the fall. Norma stood off to the side, talking with a couple of girlfriends. She saw me looking at her and motioned toward the water fountain. We walked over there together.

"Here we are," she said. She stood there, her notebook under her arm and a chewed pencil behind her ear. I had never been back to her house, although I had ridden my bike past it a half dozen times.

Holding her hair back, Norma leaned over and drank from the long pipe. She straightened and looked at me, wiping water from her mouth.

I scuffed my heels in the packed red dirt. "What are you doing this summer?" I asked.

"Going to Wilmington to stay with my grandmother."

I looked up. "But you're coming back. Right?" The words were out of my mouth before I realized it.

"I guess you'll be here this summer," she said.

I leaned over the fountain and drank tepid, rusty water. It had been months since she came to see my mother and the baby at the hospital. Norma never talked about the hospital visit, except occasionally asking how the baby was. We continued sitting next to each other in class, knowing what we did yet somehow getting beyond it. Mostly we discussed the problems at hand—fractions, difficult spelling words, the chief exports of South American countries.

Norma and I lingered at the fountain, taking turns drinking as if we had never been so thirsty. We watched classmates scatter in various directions—some on foot, some on bikes, and some in their mothers' cars. Neither of us wanted to say good-bye.

Norma bent down and plucked a dandelion. "You never gave your daddy that book, did you?"

"I keep meaning to," I said. I had hidden the copy of *Walden* in my room at the back of my bookshelf. I wasn't sure why. After all, my father knew about Norma. It wasn't as if giving it to him would reveal anything more. Sometimes I leafed through it, touching the pages my grandfather and great-grandfather had touched. I didn't know much about my forefathers on my father's side. My father never talked about them. Had they stayed up late into the night, typing and reading and smoking? Were they given to bouts of mysticism? And if so, was mysticism hereditary, like diabetes or a bad heart?

"Norma!" Her mother had pulled up in front of the school, waving from her Volkswagen. Norma pressed my hand, then ran toward the car.

"See you in the fall," I called after she had turned back toward her mother. I was afraid I would never see her again. I started to run after them, but Roger came up behind, saying, "Let's get out of here before somebody gives us homework."

I waited until Norma and her mother drove away. Then we looked around, seeing that most of the children were gone, while behind us school windows banged closed for the summer.

IT WAS NOT THE SAME visiting Aunt Louise and Uncle Clem in the nursing home. Autumn Care was not a terrible place, but it depressed me to walk the long, fluorescent-lighted hallways where old people in wheelchairs were parked outside their rooms. I pretended not to see them crook their fingers toward me. Aunt Louise and Uncle Clem's room was cramped and reeked of disinfectant, but it did have a view of the courtyard, where we sometimes walked.

The last day I had spent at their house was the day Uncle Clem moved into the nursing home. Aunt Louise had moved a few days earlier. Uncle Clem had asked to stay a couple of nights by himself. My parents were concerned that he might do something drastic, like burn the house down, but in the end they allowed him to stay.

On Clem's last morning there, my mother dropped me off early. I helped Clem with his ankle, then made us a breakfast of soft-boiled eggs, toast, and instant coffee. It was the first and only time I had taken care of him, and it proved to me that there was no need for them to go into the nursing home, but the adults would not see it that way.

Clem came to the table clean and shaved, dressed in his Sunday clothes, although it was Saturday. As we ate, I told him I didn't want him to go. He wiped a piece of egg from his mouth, said there came a time in every man's life when he had to make a change. He sipped his coffee, looking at me as if he wasn't the only one he was talking about. He did not appear as sad as I imagined he would. In fact, the closer the time had come, the more begrudgingly cheerful he had become. I had overheard my father tell my mother that Clem's changed attitude was the most heroic thing the old man had ever done.

After breakfast, Uncle Clem and I took one last walk through the garden. Since it wasn't even March, nothing was growing, although in the warm morning sun I could smell the dank earth—a sign that spring was not distant. I wondered if the people who had bought the house would look after the garden. I wondered if they knew about weeds, if they knew about following all the roots.

We walked to the back of the garden and had turned around when a voice called out to us from across the creek.

"You leaving."

It was Mr. Blakely. He was scraping something from a

frying pan into the little dog's dish. He set down the pan and, to my surprise, crossed the creek and made his way across the Moores' field toward us.

"Saw Miss Louise being drived away the other morning," Mr. Blakely said. He seemed to think about putting out his hand but then thought better of it. For a moment, my uncle just stared at him. Finally, Clem asked, "Did He send you?" He glanced heavenward.

"Mister Charlie?" Mr. Blakely rubbed his brow.

Uncle Clem turned his thumb toward the sky. "The man upstairs."

Mr. Blakely frowned upward.

"Hope you'll put in a good word for me," my uncle said.

Mr. Blakely whispered to me, "He not over that bite yet?"

"I suppose you're glad to see me go," Clem said, not looking at Mr. Blakely.

Mr. Blakely sniffed. "Won't be that long before my time comes, too." He looked back at his own house longingly.

"I never thanked you for helping the night the snake bit me," Clem said.

"I's always willing to help out Miss Louise," Mr. Blakely said.

Uncle Clem nodded as if he had known that.

"Give Miss Louise my regards," he said, then turned around. Clem and I followed him to the edge of the garden. We stood, watching the old man nimbly make his way back across the creek.

"You'll put in a good word for me?" Clem called to him.

Mr. Blakely raised his hand in affirmation or dismissal, I couldn't tell which, and then disappeared into his house.

We stood there looking into the Moores' empty field. I remember being surprised that I couldn't really picture the dog taking Mitchell down. Couldn't see Mitchell lying there. No blood. No body in the grass. I felt a lightening in me and a sadness, too. As awful as that last moment had been with Mitchell, it had been our final connection, our final time together. Now I had lost that as well.

We were climbing the drive when Uncle Charlie pulled up to the house in his Cadillac. He went inside to get two small boxes of Clem's belongings, while I lugged his one suitcase, which looked brand-new but must have been fifty years old. As I hoisted it into the trunk, my mother pulled up behind us in the Chevrolet. She lifted Ruth out and walked over to Clem, who was looking back at the house.

"We ready?" she asked my uncle. Her eyes were bloodshot.

Clem took the baby in his arms and pointed toward the house. "Ruthie," he said, his voice steady, "you're the last one to know the old place—the last one I built it for." The baby had fixed her eyes on him.

After Uncle Charlie and Clem drove away, my mother carried Ruth inside, and I heard them walk through the empty rooms. I stayed outside in the yard, stunned that the only others to recognize this ending were the pigeons on the roof, strutting and cooing, as if finally the place was theirs.

AFTER SUPPER, ROGER AND I rode up Pine Forest Drive, deciding to investigate reports my mother had heard that Miss Hawkins had returned from North Carolina. She had also heard that perhaps Miss Hawkins had not been living with a relative after all but had spent time in a mental hospital. Now that my mother was back at her job, she heard about things well before they ever made the paper, if they ever did—that Mill's Mill was shutting down, that a group of investors were eyeing the old Furman campus for a shopping mall, that there were plans to fluoridate Greenville's water, which would make it no longer the purest in the world.

Roger and I had left Henry in the front yard, lightning bugs rising into his cupped hands. I had almost told Roger to go on without me. Part of me had wanted to stay in the yard and keep my brother company. Henry and I were veterans of a different family, a different configuration that the baby's coming had pushed into the past.

But I was curious about Miss Hawkins, and twilight was the best time to ride bikes because there was very little traffic. Also, a cool breeze brought relief from the mid-July heat. We rode with no hands, stood on our seats, balanced on one pedal. We passed the McDaniel Heights apartments, where Roger's father didn't live anymore. After the divorce was final, he had moved across town. Every weekend, Dr. Avant took Roger to a movie or on an afternoon hike. Sometimes I watched Dr. Avant walk up the drive and ring the doorbell. Trudy Avant would come out on the porch, and they would talk civilly—at least it looked civil from across the street.

When Roger and I reached Miss Hawkins's street, we slowed. We pulled up in front of her house, seeing that her lights were on.

"It's true," Roger said.

"Maybe this isn't such a good idea," I said, looking around, expecting Miss Hawkins to jump out of the nandinas, brandishing a thick ruler.

"Come on." Roger laid his bike against the curb, then I

set mine down. We tiptoed through the uncut grass of her side yard.

Something cold nuzzled my hand. It was her dog, wagging its tail as if it remembered us. We crept through the bushes, which had grown ragged. We peeked in the window. A lamp was on and a book was open on a table. There was a tray with cookies, several teacups, and a steaming teapot.

"Looks like she is expecting somebody," I said.

"She probably went out to the kitchen." Roger tried to look off to the side. "Maybe we ought to go around to get a better look." When we turned around, standing behind us in the faint lamplight, was Miss Hawkins, who didn't seem quite as towering.

"How are you boys?" Her face looked softer, and when she talked her voice didn't have its old edge. "Won't you come in?"

"We better be getting home," Roger said.

"We have to be back before dark," I chimed in.

"I am sure your parents wouldn't mind if you spent a few moments with your old teacher." She led us around through the kitchen door, the one that had swung open on its own last November.

She led us into the living room, the dog following. The room smelled of peppermint and something sour, which I realized was a litter box. The Siamese was curled on the sofa. I noticed the framed photograph that I had broken was back on the mantel, the glass taped.

We sat at the table that held the tea service. Miss Hawkins petted the dog, which was curled at her feet, and then she filled our teacups. She passed us milk and sugar, then the plate of cookies. When I took three, she frowned, and I put two back.

She turned to Roger. "Your father divorced your mother."

Roger looked into his lap.

"I'm sorry" was all she said. Her tone was mellow. She seemed tired, like someone recuperating.

Miss Hawkins looked at me. "And you have a baby sister?"

"Yes, ma'am." I sipped my tea.

Miss Hawkins sipped her tea, too. The Siamese rubbed against her leg, and a clock in the other room ticked. Roger and I looked at each other, wondering if we were expected to introduce something into the conversation. Roger's contribution was to pick up his teacup and take a long, loud sip. I found my gaze wandering back to the photograph on the mantel. I cleared my throat again and heard myself ask, "And how have you been, Miss Hawkins?" The question sounded idiotic once I had asked it, especially if what my mother had heard was true.

"Better." She took another sip of tea. "I regret leaving the class in the lurch, although Evelyn Watts is an excellent teacher." Her teacup rattled in its saucer from her shaking. She looked at me. "How is Norma?"

I sat up, surprised she would consider me someone to ask about Norma. "She's in Wilmington with her grandmother." I had received several postcards from her and had written back on Howard Johnson postcards.

"She was the most intelligent girl I have ever taught. She and your mother, Jeru." She held out the plate to me. I hesitated, then took a cookie. I had known my mother was smart but not that smart.

When it was time to leave, Miss Hawkins walked us to the kitchen door, shook our hands, and asked us to come see her. It was a cordial visit, eventful in its uneventfulness. We did not visit her again, though, no longer needing her to name our losses.

ON A VERY HOT FRIDAY AFTERNOON, Della and I rode the bus downtown, where we were to meet my family at the S&W Cafeteria. My mother had taken the afternoon off and gone shopping with the baby and Henry. I preferred to spend the afternoon sloshing up the middle of a muddy creek with Roger rather than trying on stiff new clothes. That my mother didn't make me go was another benefit of the baby; Ruth was too much work for my mother to spend much time insisting I do anything.

My father was out of town on a business trip, so my mother made me agree to ride with Della later in the afternoon and meet them at the cafeteria for supper.

The bus was sweltering, even with all the windows down. The bus driver had a little fan on the dashboard, but whatever breeze it created petered out before it got to Della and me, who sat in the back, among her friends. Della was wearing a bright, silky purple blouse, a black skirt, long dangly earrings, and so many bracelets that she sounded like a wind chime every time she moved. Her bracelets were a barometer of her emotional state, and since she was as relieved about my mother and the birth as I was, she had been wearing a lot of bracelets lately.

I looked out at the passing neighborhoods and thought I was seldom alone with Della any more, since she spent much of her day looking after the baby. The bus had left the tree-lined neighborhoods and was taking us over the

Church Street bridge that led downtown. On the left was downtown and on the right was Springwood.

Della checked her watch. "It's a little early to meet your mama." She started to pull the cord but hesitated. "You want to pull it?"

"Here?" I looked around, seeing we were several blocks from the Dollar Store or the cafeteria. I tugged the cord that rang the bell, and the driver pulled over at the next stop. It wasn't until we had stepped off the bus that I realized we were standing at the entrance to Springwood.

"I thought we would pay Mitchell a visit this afternoon," Della said, hitching her pocketbook onto her shoulder and starting through the wrought-iron gates.

I didn't move.

"Well now, Jeru," she said, smiling gently. "We don't have to go in there. I know your mama hasn't been coming by as much as she would like. I thought he might be lonely."

It was true. My mother hadn't had time to stop by Mitchell's grave as often. And although my father had never visited the grave as far as I knew, he did seem to refer less to Mitchell. I, too, had thought less about him. We weren't trying to forget Mitchell, but the baby demanded all our attention. Even mine. Especially when Della let me give Ruth a bath or feed her a bottle.

"Well?" Della stood with her hands on her hips.

"OK," I said, and followed her through the gates and into the shade of several old oaks. Little streets curved in and out of what seemed like thousands and thousands of grave markers. I stopped. "I don't know where he's buried." I had been there only the few times with my mother.

Della took my hand and, without even looking around, led me down one of the little streets that wound around and then toward a hill. We passed by a tent with three rows of fold-up chairs set out beside a newly dug grave, but no one was around. I ran to the edge. Standing beside the mound of red dirt, I peeked over the edge, my heart pounding. It was empty. A deep rectangular hole.

I studied the slick red sides of the grave and smelled the freshly dug dirt. It reminded me of when Clem plowed his garden each spring; he said he was turning over the beds, and I always wanted to spend a night in one, sleeping between the furrowed rows. And if dying was like that, like sleeping in my uncle's garden, smelling sweet dirt all the time, then maybe it wasn't so bad.

I followed Della up the hill and then along a slight ridge, markers all around us. Beyond them and the tall iron fence was downtown. We could hear the traffic, which had picked up because people were getting off work at department stores and law offices and hotels. And some people were coming into town for supper or to see a movie. But here in Springwood it was quiet, except for the crickets' urgent song.

Finally, we came to the family plot, which looked like all the other plots, with some new markers and some old. I don't know what I was expecting, some kind of family resemblance in stone.

"I stops by now and then to see him." Della brushed a stick and some leaves off the little mound that was Mitchell's grave. She had never said anything about coming to the cemetery.

I knelt beside Mitchell's headstone, which looked too new. I pressed my hands against the engraved letters of his

name and felt the stone's warmth. I walked across my relatives' graves, reading the worn markers of grandparents
and great-grandparents, great-aunts and great-uncles.
There was really nothing here about Mitchell or Grandma
Grace or Grandpa Jeru or any of these other relatives except the date they were born and the date they died and a
line that was the life connecting the two.

Della sat on a bench off to the side and lit a cigarette. I
sat beside her, and we looked at the Greenville skyline,
which was mostly shadow now. I was a little afraid she
might become hysterical since the only other time I had
been here with her was at the funeral itself, when she had
thrown herself onto his coffin. She sat calmly, serenely
smoking her Kool. And whatever her reason for bringing
me, it felt good to be here with her, without the preacher
and the hearse and the cars strung out behind with their
headlights burning as if it were the middle of the night.

"He was a sweet, sweet boy," she said, nodding to the
grave. "But I didn't loves him any more than I loves you."
She put her arm around me and drew me against her, and
I felt something change in me. This was the first time that
I knew, really knew, that Mitchell's death had not less-
ened who he had been, and, in knowing this, I released
him, gave him up. And although I was getting to the age
where this kind of open affection made me uncomfortable, I stayed next to Della.

After a while, she said it was time to meet my mother,
and we walked back through the darkening cemetery, out
the gates, and then a few blocks until we were standing in
front of the S&W Cafeteria. We found my mother waiting
in the bright lobby with the baby in her arms and Henry
at her side.

I remember wanting Della to come into the dining room with us, which I knew was an impossibility. Negroes might cook and even serve behind the line, but only whites ate at the S&W. Still, I think my mother and Henry must have wished the same thing, to stay in her company. We all turned to Della.

"I'm meeting friends," Della said, which might have been true but which she would have said anyway. She was practiced in saving our feelings. She waved good-bye and disappeared through the swishing revolving door, leaving us to fend for ourselves.

CHAPTER THIRTEEN

The Cabin

IT WAS THE FIRST SUNDAY RIDE in some time that did not feel like an afternoon excursion into what was wrong with us. Although it had been raining steadily all morning, after lunch my father suggested we go for a ride. We protested, but he broke out the umbrellas, herded us to the car, and drove us into the mountains.

He shifted smoothly into second gear as our new Biscayne breezed up the incline, passing a stalled car at the side of the road. The wipers squeaked on the new windshield. My father smiled at something he said to himself, a lit cigarette bobbing in the corner of his mouth.

"Where are you taking us?" My mother stroked Ruth's head as she slept in her lap. Henry and I stared out at the cloud-shrouded mountains. Earlier, Henry had looked at me and shrugged, wondering what we all were wondering—why had our father dragged us out in such dreary weather?

He drove with his arm draped over the steering wheel, mumbling something else. Ever since he had gone back to work, he talked more to himself, but it wasn't the troubled kind of muttering he had done before the baby came. It sounded calming, more like a chant. Perhaps it was part of the way he handled going back to work, dealing with clients, writing things he didn't want to write. To help him cope with his outer world, his inner world had become louder.

"What is this about?" My mother looked out the window as the car skirted the white guardrails, all that was between us and a hundred-foot drop.

My father scratched his chin; his afternoon shadow was already growing out.

"You kill me." My mother laughed. The baby opened her eyes but then slowly shut them again, her little chest rising and falling. My mother lowered her voice. "Why do you make things so mysterious?"

"I don't make them mysterious," he said, tapping his cigarette in the ashtray. "They just are." He glanced at her, no trace of a smile. "Besides, what is so mysterious about a Sunday-afternoon ride?"

"We can't see a thing." My mother nodded at the blurred windshield, which yielded views only between passes of the wipers, and even then most of what we saw was rain. My mother settled back against the seat, seeming content not to know. This was the difference I had noticed in both my parents after the baby was born. Things that might have bothered them before, irritations that might have sparked full-fledged arguments, seemed to defuse themselves. My parents had regained a kind of momentum that made them less susceptible to bickering and irritations. And for Henry and me, this meant that no longer did we hang on our parents' every word, no longer was our family up for discussion.

The new Biscayne glided to the top of Caesar's Head. Henry and I rubbed our hands over the shiny new upholstery and leaned forward, watching the second hand sweep around on the dashboard clock. All of our previous cars had had a blank place where the clock should have been.

My father had called my mother from his office two nights ago, saying he had to work late, and an hour later pulled in front of the house with this new car. When my mother asked if we could afford it, he said he had gotten a raise for doing such a good job on the Texize account. He had been working weekends and more late nights at the office, sometimes not getting home until we were in bed. My mother never mentioned money any more.

The rain slackened as we drove past the lookout tower and down the other side of Caesar's Head. I remembered how our car had broken down last fall and how my father had disappeared. He was changed. I couldn't picture him vanishing in an angry cloud of steam.

He pulled down a winding gravel road that led to the tin-roofed cabin we had always admired from the road, the cabin with a pond below it, the cabin where my father said Thoreau might like to live.

"What are you doing?" My mother sat up.

"Getting a closer look." He drove down the oak-lined driveway that skirted the pond, the gravel popping underneath our tires, and then drove on up to the cabin and turned off the engine.

My mother lifted the baby out of her lap and set her on her shoulder so that she was looking back at us. The baby yawned.

"I thought we might walk around." My father started to get out of the car.

"Won't the owners mind?"

"Good question." My father put out his cigarette. "Do you mind?"

"What are you talking about?" my mother asked.

"Well, it's not ours yet, but the guy has offered me a very good deal . . ."

"This place?"

"It is not the Keys."

My mother looked up at the cabin. It had cedar siding stained a dark green so that it was camouflaged by two shaggy Norway spruces. The house looked dingier and neglected up close. "First a new car"—my mother rubbed the dashboard—"and now a cabin. What has come over you?"

"Materialism." My father leaned back in his seat.

"This is going to be our place?" Henry was beside himself. He leaped out of the car and raced down to the pond. I followed after him to the pond's edge. The rain made it look like a thousand fish were kissing the water.

"Be careful, boys," my mother called after us as they got out of the car and went up to the front door. My father produced a single key from the inside of his coat pocket, fit it in the lock, and pushed open the door.

"You are serious," I heard my mother say as they walked on in, my father carrying Ruth.

Henry and I walked onto the dock, where a johnboat half-filled with rainwater was tied. Bullfrogs bellowed in the rain, water spiders skated across the surface, and every now and then a fish slapped the water. A huge beech tree leaned out over the pond, initials with plus signs between them carved in its smooth bark. I had often pictured myself on just such a dock, a cane pole in my hands, pulling in plate-sized bream.

Henry bent down and swished his fingers in the tea-colored water. I squatted beside him, holding his shirt to make sure he didn't fall in. We stayed there for a little while, looking down into the water and hoping a monstrous dream fish might swim by.

There was a loud clap of thunder. Henry and I ran up the path to the house, reaching the front stoop as the rain began to pour again, drumming the tin roof. Although there were windows, it was fairly dark inside. My father tried a light switch, but from the looks of things the electricity had not been on in some time.

"He said he would sell it to me furnished." My father wiped dust off a broken recliner with his handkerchief and sat Ruth in it. "Such as it is."

It was a simple cabin with a kitchen, a den with a fireplace, and two bedrooms with bunk beds. It smelled molded and mildewy, no one having been here in years. The walls watched us with eyes of knotted pine. There were bookshelves beside the fireplace with Reader's Digest books, a few jigsaw puzzles of New England scenes, and a rattlesnake skin that, when Henry held it up over his head, still touched the ground. "Wonder if they found this around here," he said, his eyes wide.

My father tried to open a couple of windows, banging them with the heel of his hand, but they were painted shut. "It isn't in the greatest shape." He glanced upward at the rain still drumming on the roof. "At least there aren't any leaks."

My mother ran her finger along the kitchen counter,

then smiled at my father. I couldn't tell if she liked the house. I could tell my father couldn't tell either. He strained to open a window.

"You don't want a mountain cabin to be too nice." She opened the old rusted refrigerator that looked a lot like Aunt Louise's.

"The guy said there is a screened-in porch you can't see from the road." My father started for the back door. "He claimed there is a view."

Henry had found an empty hornets' nest on one shelf. I thumbed through a yellowed copy of *Boys' Life*. I was trying not to get excited, knowing that the more enthusiastic you were around adults, the less likely it was they would do what you wanted.

My father tugged on the back door. "They painted this shut too." He rummaged through the kitchen drawers and came back with a screwdriver. He worked it between the door and the doorjamb, and finally the door popped open. There was a rush of fresh air and the smell of rain. The cabin was lighter and, with the door open, seemed a very different place.

We walked onto the porch.

"The view is a big cloud." Henry pressed his nose against the screen. All we could see were gray cotton wisps of rain clouds.

My mother sat in a rocker with Ruth. My father leaned back in a chair against the wall, and Henry and I climbed into a swing at the far end of the porch. Its rusty chain creaked when we kicked our legs. This moment, on the back porch of a house that didn't belong to us, was the first time since Mitchell's death that we felt at home together.

I watched our mother holding the baby. I thought how wrong I had been to fear Ruth's coming. It had, in fact, returned our mother to us.

"Smell that mountain air," my mother said.

"Smells like our basement," Henry said.

"The air is ours if we want it." My father held out his arms, embracing the air. His face had softened since he had gone back to the agency—not reflecting defeat as much as acceptance.

It gradually stopped raining. The clouds lifted in layers until we were blinking in the sunlight. With the clouds gone, we could see the backyard was an open meadow and beyond it, framed between Fraser firs, was a long view of mountains behind mountains, like frozen waves. For months now, mushroom clouds had been conspicuously absent from my horizons.

"Like a postcard," my mother said, which made me think of Norma and the postcards I had been sending her. I thought how even if we did buy this place, she would not be able to enjoy it and how that was not right. It didn't seem fair that the absence or presence of your parents should determine what you could have and what you could not. I didn't want the house. I didn't want anything that would bring me pleasure, because whatever it was, it wouldn't rightfully be mine.

My father stood and breathed deeply. "I thought it would be handy to have a place to get away with the children." He picked up Ruth and blew against her stomach. She squealed. He touched her nose. "Maybe in twenty years, after you and your brothers have gone off to college, I'll come up here and write." He lifted her in his arms, pushed open the screen door, and we followed him out into the yard. "Not to mention, it is a good investment."

My mother put her hand around my father's waist as they walked through the meadow. Henry and I ran a little ahead. Ponderous June bugs buzzed lazily around us, running into our legs and tumbling into the grass. Henry picked one up and threw it into the air, watching it fly. "They don't pay attention where they're going."

We stopped at a rushing creek, full from the rain. Henry and I took off our shoes and waded down a little from our parents. The water was cold and clear.

"Be careful," our mother called.

Henry stooped down into the water, fearlessly turning over stones and pushing back the high grass.

"I bet we don't buy this place," I whispered to Henry.

Our parents sat on rocks by the creek. My father was watching my mother. "Something is bothering you," he said.

"I don't know." My mother leaned over the water, picking up a smooth stone. "It makes me nervous."

"What?" My father's face went slack, and I heard a hint of desperation in his tone. Ruth cooed in his arms.

"To buy our dream house. Seems risky." My mother threw the stone, making a plunking noise. "Who knows what might happen here."

"Exactly," my father said.

"I told you," I whispered to Henry who was engrossed in a salamander he had found under a rock.

I got out, because the water was freezing, but Henry waded on down the creek. I sat on the bank, watching him.

"We can't not do things because we are afraid of what

might happen," my father said, stroking Ruth's cheek. "Where's your faith?"

My mother plucked a piece of grass and pressed it between her hands. She put her cupped hands to her mouth and blew, making a long, low whistle. I had noticed that *Science and Health* stayed on the bookshelf now. And the last time I had had a cold, she offered me aspirin rather than quotations. For my mother, religion had been a refuge, a resting place, a hiatus from life. For my father, religion was life.

Henry hopped out of the creek and ran toward us, holding up something that wriggled wildly in his hand. He held it out toward my mother, thinking he might scare her.

But it was my father who backed away with the baby. "Is it poisonous?"

"Just a little water snake," my mother said, taking it in her hands. The snake stopped wriggling, as if it sensed a kindred spirit. She let it lie on her arm, running her finger along its back. "I was always finding these in Clem's garden when I was a little girl."

"Can I keep it?" Henry asked, stroking the snake with his finger.

My mother shook her head, handing the snake back to Henry. "We can't keep what we don't own."

Henry sighed, carrying it back to its place beside the creek, letting it slither off into the grass. My father's head fell as if he understood what my mother was saying.

"I suppose we could come visit the snake now and then." My mother turned to my father.

My father sat up, squinting at her.

Henry and I looked at each other.

"And since we're going to be coming up here anyway," my mother said, taking the baby from my father, "we might as well buy this place."

Doing his best to keep a straight face, my father said, "Might as well."

It wasn't elation I felt, but then neither was it the guilt I had anticipated. I walked back to the house alone to try to resee what was about to be ours. In the kitchen, I ran my hand over the old kettle on the stove and imagined its lively whistling. I found a yardstick from Mackey's Funeral Home propped next to the fireplace and walked around tapping the floor, the walls, the rusted horseshoe over the front door. In one of the tiny bedrooms, I sat on a lower bunk bed, testing squeaky springs. I swung my legs onto the bare mattress, laid back, and, putting my hands behind my head, thought of all the boys who had lain here before me, listening to rainwater drain through the downspout.

I WAS DEEP IN THE COOKIE SECTION of the Eight O'Clock Superette, examining a package of Marshmallow Pinwheels, when I felt a hand on my shoulder. I turned and found Norma there with a cart full of groceries. She was tanned, maybe a little taller, and there was something else different that took me a minute to comprehend: She was wearing a bra. I could see its outline, like two small lemons, beneath her blouse.

Her mother was farther down the aisle in the cereal section.

"Thanks for the postcards," she said. Maybe it was the bra or maybe it was an awkwardness that came with her growing into a new body. Whatever the reason, she didn't seem quite like her old, comfortable self. The summer had put a new distance between us.

A mother with a small boy pushed passed us, her cart stacked with canned goods and frozen foods. The wooden floors of the Eight O'Clock creaked and groaned. I had been coming here with my mother since I was a baby.

"How's Ruth?" asked Norma.

I shrugged, glancing at her mother down the aisle. She was sifting through a box of coupons and hadn't seen me.

Norma held up a fat packet of notebook paper in her cart. "Can you believe school starts in one week?" She looked around then took a step closer to me, whispering in my ear. "Miss Hawkins is in the store somewhere." She put her finger to her lip. "Rolled her cart right past me." We heard the rattle of a cart coming around the corner.

"Have you picked out the cookies you want?" It was my mother, her cart filled with packages wrapped in butcher paper. I set the Marshmallow Pinwheels in the cart as my mother, smiling at Norma, asked, "Were you away this summer?"

Norma stepped back, as if my mother had caught us doing something, but then regained her composure. "I was at my grandmother's in Wilmington." She stood there a minute more, glanced at me, and then started to push her cart down the aisle. Her mother had seen us, and while I could tell she was debating whether she should speak to us, my mother recognized her.

"How are you, Mrs. Jones?" My mother held out her hand to Norma's mother.

"I'm well," she said, a little coolly. "Norma tells me congratulations are in order. A new baby girl."

Norma and I found ourselves backed against the canned-soup section.

My mother folded up her shopping list and put it in her purse. "She's at home with my husband." She looked at her watch. "Which reminds me, we have to hurry. He is a little uncertain of himself with babies."

Mrs. Jones gave a little grunt. "Tell me about it."

My mother looked up at her. Norma and I backed all the way to the rice section.

"I mean," said Mrs. Jones, her tone softening a little, "that my husband was the same way."

My mother smiled cautiously at Mrs. Jones, but Mrs. Jones did not smile back; then we said good-bye and went our separate ways.

"What an odd little woman." My mother stopped and watched Norma and her mother walk down the aisle in the other direction. "Wilmington." She looked at me. "Who else lives in Wilmington?"

I shrugged, something I had found myself doing more. I was entering the age of shrugs. It wasn't until she had tipped the bag boy and had gotten in the car that my mother hit the steering wheel with her palm, and I knew she had made the connection. She put the key in the ignition but didn't turn it. She sat back and looked at me. "It's Norma. Isn't it?"

I looked out the window.

"That's why she came to the hospital." She pointed her finger at me. "You have known all along."

I shrugged.

Hearing a rattle, we saw a bag boy pushing a grocery cart for Miss Hawkins, who walked behind. We both slunk down in our seats.

"She says you and Norma are the smartest students she ever had," I said after Miss Hawkins had passed and was unlocking her trunk for the bag boy.

"You're changing the subject," my mother said.

We watched Miss Hawkins rummage in her purse for a tip.

"Your father knows too," my mother said. She looked at me again. "You told him." She started the car, and as we pulled out of the parking lot she touched my shoulder. "There is so much you haven't been able to say."

A MONTH AFTER SCHOOL HAD STARTED, in the middle of a cool October night, I woke to the sound of a trash can being banged around. Probably a possum or a raccoon in the garbage, but I was too sleepy to get up, so I rolled over. The sound stopped. All I could hear was the tick of Aunt Louise's mantel clock on my bookshelf.

I was almost asleep when I heard it again. From my bed I saw light flicker in the window. I went to my window and looked out on the back drive. I saw a small fire contained within a trash can, and my father was feeding sheets of paper into it.

In my pajamas, I tiptoed past Henry's room, past the nursery and my parents' bedroom, then down the basement steps, through the open doors of the office and outside.

My father cradled a stack of sheets in his arm. "Doing a little housecleaning," he said, as if he had been expecting me.

"In the middle of the night?" I looked up at the clear night sky. The moon was out. Dead leaves rattled in the trees.

My father put his arm around me. "I finally finished."

"Finished what?" I yawned, rubbing sleep out of my eyes.

"My book." He fed another sheet into the fire and nodded to the flaming pages in the trash can. "Decided you had the right idea."

"You're burning it?" I started to reach into the fire, but he held my arm back.

My father's face was lit by the fire. "Tibetan monks spend months making complicated sand designs—"

"—and then they set them on the mountainside and let them get blown away. I know. You have told me that. But your book. All that work!"

"Oh, no, no, no." He smiled as he stirred the fire with a stick, then dropped in the rest of the pages. "These are only notes." He watched the fire.

"Oh," I said, relieved.

Just to make sure, I peeked inside his open office door and saw a tall, neat stack of pages, spotlighted by his desk lamp. I flipped through the pages, impressed by all that typing. I started to read the first page, but something made me stop. Perhaps I was afraid of being disappointed or that I wouldn't understand. I went back out and stood beside him. Now he was holding a shoe box filled with blue letters.

"Jeru? Warren?" My mother stood silhouetted in the basement doorway, her arms crossed over her robe, her hair in curlers. "What are y'all doing out here?" She joined us by the fire.

"I finished." My father hugged her. "I finally finished."

"That is wonderful. Where is it?"

He poked the flaming sheets with his piece of pipe.

"Oh, Warren." She put her hand to her mouth. She pulled away from him, her eyes shone.

"The book is inside." He patted her shoulder. "These are notes." He dumped the shoe box of letters into the fire.

"Mama? Daddy?" Henry came out of the basement door. He had on his pajamas, and he dragged his stuffed elephant by its nose. "What are we doing out here?" He came over and stood against my mother.

"Celebrating," my father said, patting Henry's head.

With everyone looking at Henry, I pulled a typed sheet from the edge of the trash can. I held the singed page up to the flickering light and read, "He dreams again of his children. He dreams and he does not sleep. They are all with him in the dream—all of them—all healthy, all alive, all under one roof. He dreams and he does not sleep." There were notes scribbled in the margin that I couldn't make out. I folded the page and put it in my pajama pocket.

"It's cold out here," Henry said, moving beside me, closer to the fire. We stood there, until the flames began to die. The cat's eyes glowed in the bushes.

"Are there clouds at night, but you just can't see them?" Henry asked, looking up into the black sky.

"What now, Warren?" My mother watched my father.

He looked at her.

Henry and I stood at the edge of the fire and watched the pages burn. I ran back inside, up the basement stairs and into my room. Shoving aside the biographies, I reached to the back of the shelf for my father's hidden copy of *Walden*. I held it in my hands and looked out the window at the fire, whose light contained my family yet made everything around them dark.

I started back down the stairs with the book but was stopped by a harrowing cry from Mitchell's room. The baby, like the rest of us, was awake.

ABOUT THE AUTHOR

TOMMY HAYS grew up in Greenville, South Carolina, and was educated at Furman University and the MFA Program for Writers at Warren Wilson College. His first novel was *Sam's Crossing.* He teaches at the University of North Carolina at Asheville and lives with his wife and two children.

ABOUT THE TYPE

This book was set in Garth Graphic, a typeface designed by Renée LeWinter and Connie Blanchard around 1976. It is based on a font called Matt Antique, designed by John Matt in the mid-1960s for American Typefounders' phototypesetter. The present font was developed by the Compugraphic Corporation and was named for the firm's cofounder William W. Garth, Jr.